OBSESSION – A CRIME OF THE HEART

NOIR NIGHTS BOOK 3

ROBIN STOREY

Cover design by Candy Lyn Thomen
Formatting by Polgarus Studio

For Aaron

CHAPTER 1

Benny slipped his arm through the louvre and twisted it around to reach the handle on the back door. He popped the button to unlock it, opened it and slipped inside. He was in the laundry, the size of a large cupboard.

In all the years he'd been doing this, he could never get over how easy it was. Sometimes it seemed as if the occupants were inviting him to break in. Especially these workers' cottages. The owners spent a small fortune renovating them, then either ran out of money or decided that because they lived in a trendy suburb, they didn't need to bother with security.

Benny stepped over a mound of dirty washing into a short hallway and then into the living room. The exterior of the weatherboard cottage, painted in white with blue trim, looked fresh and new, but inside it was a different story.

The walls were stained with mould and plastered patches, and the sagging couch was almost hidden by the piles of clothes flung over it. A large screen TV on the wall looked down on a table overflowing with empty pizza boxes and beer cans. The room smelled of stale food and clothes. It was easy to see that a man lived here. No woman would put up with this mess.

Benny wandered into the kitchen. Scuffed linoleum floor, grease marks on the wall behind the stove and grubby lace curtains over the window. The sink was full of dirty dishes and fruit flies wafted around two overripe bananas on the bench.

In the pantry was a small jar of Vegemite and two tins of baked beans. Benny opened the refrigerator door. A half loaf of bread, half a soggy tomato, a jar of pickles and a block of cheese. In the freezer, a tray of ice cubes—not even a tub of ice cream. Disappointing.

He continued down the tiny hallway, poking his head into the bathroom. Drab, grotty shower, wet towels on the floor. Then two bedrooms. In the first, an exercise bike surrounded by piles of unopened boxes. In the second was an unmade bed, the covers thrown back. The sheets looked as if they hadn't been changed for weeks and the room stank of body odour.

The small bedside table was piled high with more dirty dishes and cups. On the wall was another large screen TV, with a PlayStation gaming console underneath. So the guy was young, as well as single. Or if he had a girlfriend, he certainly didn't bring her back here.

Benny returned to the kitchen. His stomach was rumbling; he'd have to make do with what was in the fridge. He opened all the cupboard doors until he found a toaster and plugged it in.

He took out the loaf of bread and the cheese from the fridge and popped two slices of bread into the toaster. He found a knife and a plate, and as there was no butter, spread the toast liberally with Vegemite. He slid the cheese out of the packet, cut off all the hard, mouldy bits and placed a couple of slices on top of the Vegemite.

After putting everything away, he wandered back into the living room with his snack. He moved all the clothes to one end of the couch and sat down. He found the remote control under a pair of underpants and turned on the TV, scrolling through the channels.

No pay TV. The guy could afford to live in Newtown and only had free to air? Benny had forgotten to check if there was a satellite dish on the roof before he broke in. Another disappointment. He couldn't afford pay TV at home, and he loved nothing more than settling down on a stranger's couch, turning on the Movie Channel and finding a movie starring Errol Flynn, John Wayne or Clint Eastwood, his three favourite actors. He always imagined himself as the hero, killing the baddies and saving the girl.

As he munched on his toast, Benny watched the shopping channel. An excited woman in gym gear was talking about the Miracle Ab Exerciser. Usually these shows made him feel that he instantly needed whatever it was they were advertising, but in this case, not so much.

The woman made it look easy, but he knew it wasn't. Years ago, his Auntie Rose had one, and by the time she'd reached fifty, she was red in the face and sweating.

On the table in front of him was an untidy pile of magazines. A couple on gaming, and underneath, a pile of magazines called Tits and Arses. Benny picked one up. On the cover was a topless woman with breasts like giant watermelons and nipples like headlights. Her tongue poked out over her luscious red lips and she was looking at Benny as if she wanted to eat him. He turned the pages, aroused, but at the same time, prickling with shame.

He remembered the first time he'd ever seen one of these magazines. He was only six and living with Auntie Vi. He found a pile of magazines under the bed in the spare room, and flicked through them, horrified, yet unable to stop looking at the women, at their smooth, tanned skin and pink, glistening bits. Auntie Vi caught him and gave him the strap.

'How dare you!' she raged, 'That's private property, they're Uncle Russell's magazines.'

Benny had never heard her mention Uncle Russell and was too afraid to ask any further. When he told Auntie Fran about it years later, she laughed. She had a low, husky laugh, as if she'd smoked too many cigarettes, although she didn't smoke.

'Honey, there's no Uncle Russell. The magazines are Auntie Vi's. She's a closet lesbian, even though she won't admit it. '

Benny put the magazine down and to take his mind off his discomfort, wandered into the bedroom again. He opened the wardrobe door. A couple of shirts on hangers and the rest of his clothes—jeans, polo shirts and t-shirts—were folded in messy heaps on the shelves. Nothing formal. Perhaps he was in one of those marketing or IT jobs where you could wear jeans to work and drink coffee and lie around in bean bags. He'd seen a show about them on TV.

He went over to the bedside table and wrenched open the top drawer. Socks and underwear. Second drawer the same. The bottom drawer overflowed with bits and pieces and paperwork.

He pulled out an envelope addressed to Joshua Anderson, 12 Waterloo Street, Newtown. Inside was a letter from Your Home Property Management.

'Dear Joshua, You are advised that there will be an inspection of your rental property on Saturday 5 November.'

Benny had to read it slowly to understand it. The date was over two months ago; he should have picked his time better. He should have broken in after Joshua had tidied the house for the inspection.

He put the letter back and spied a leather cover peeking out from a pile of burger wrappings on the bedside table. He eased it out. It was an iPad. He opened it and swiped. Up came the homepage. Brilliant, no password needed. Perhaps he might learn something interesting about Joshua Anderson.

He took the iPad into the living room, flopped on the couch with his feet up on the coffee table and started scrolling through the various pages.

As far as emails went, Joshua didn't get many. Someone had replied to one he'd sent and his signature at the bottom read, 'Joshua Anderson, Software developer, Whoosh Development and Design.'

Benny gave an inward whoop of triumph. He was right about Joshua being in IT. Then again, he was pretty good at learning things about people from breaking into their homes; he'd had plenty of experience.

He scrolled through Joshua's Facebook feed, which consisted mostly of posts from gaming groups. He couldn't find a mention anywhere of a girlfriend. Perhaps Joshua didn't want one, or maybe he was too into gaming to bother. Or perhaps he did want one, but wasn't having any luck. If so, Benny could sympathise with him.

He put the iPad back on the bedside table, then took his plate into the kitchen. Chances were that if he put the plate in the sink with others, Joshua would never notice. But out of habit, because he always left every house exactly as he found it, he rinsed the plate, dried it with the grubby tea towel hanging on the oven door and put it back in the cupboard.

He went out through the laundry, locking the door behind him. He certainly wouldn't be coming back here again.

#

4

On the bus home to Marrickville, Benny thought about Joshua Anderson. His life seemed to revolve around gaming, eating junk food and drinking. Pretty sad. The house had made him feel depressed—it looked inviting from the outside, but inside it was crap. You could never tell by looking at the outside. Just like people.

Benny didn't break and enter to steal things, although he had done it as a sideline when he was a teenager. But after being caught trying to sell some stolen jewellery, appearing in court and have the magistrate threaten to send him to jail, he decided it wasn't worth the trouble. He broke into houses to make himself feel good, to peek into another person's life, pretend he was someone else for a few hours. Technically, he supposed that eating someone's food was stealing, but he told himself it was different if they didn't know.

He wondered again about Joshua's love life. Even if he didn't have a girlfriend now, he'd probably had one in the past. He guessed that Joshua was younger than him, probably in his twenties, so there wasn't a lot of shame at that age in admitting that you didn't have a girlfriend.

When you got to 42, though, people started to think that you were a bit strange. Benny had often been asked if he was gay. And that always upset him—not that people might think he was gay, but thinking there could be no other reason that he didn't have a girlfriend.

Women usually reacted to him in one of two ways. They either ignored him, or looked at him with pity, as if he was some freak who'd grown an extra head. Once on the bus, he'd got chatting to the girl beside him and told her that Errol Flynn was his favourite actor in the whole world.

'Cool!' she exclaimed. 'It's so unusual to meet someone who likes those old movies.'

But when Benny asked her if she'd like to come to his house to watch his favourite Errol Flynn movie, The Adventures of Robin Hood, she tossed her head and snorted, 'As if,' got up and moved to another seat. So she'd lied— she didn't think it was cool after all.

The bus screeched to a stop. A young girl got on with a folded up stroller in one hand and a whingeing toddler in a pink dress on her hip. Benny sprang up, took the stroller from her and put it in the luggage rack. She sat down beside him, placing the toddler on her knee, and smiled at him.

'Thank you so much.'

The toddler stared at Benny, stopped grizzling and gave him a wide toothy grin. Benny blew a raspberry at her and she giggled. The more raspberries he blew, the harder she giggled. He loved the sound of children laughing; it was pure and full of joy. They couldn't put it on, not like adults.

The passengers in the surrounding seats were smiling; it was infectious, like a disease, but in a good way. The girl laughed as well. 'You're good with kids, she's usually wary of strangers.'

'I love kids,' Benny said.

He remembered when he was 15 telling Auntie Fran, the last time he went to live with her, that one day he would get married and have lots of kids. Auntie Fran was sitting at the kitchen table after her shower doing her nails. She leaned back to survey her handiwork, her robe gaping open to reveal the swell of a breast and a glimpse of flat, pearly white stomach. Benny swallowed hard and crossed his legs.

'That's wonderful!' Aunt Fran said. 'You'd be a perfect father, you're just a big kid yourself.'

The way she'd said it, it was a good thing to be a big kid. Not like at school when the teacher wrote on his report card that he was 'childlike' and the other kids called him Dumbo.

Shortly after he started school, the principal told Auntie Vi he thought Benny would be better off in a special school. When Auntie Fran heard about it, she drove all the way from Sydney to see the principal, and tell him there was no way her nephew was going to a special school. It was discrimination and if they weren't prepared to accept him she'd take them to court.

That night at home, he overheard her talking to Auntie Vi over a glass of wine on the patio.

'So how did you persuade him?' Auntie Vi asked.

'I told you, threatened to take them to court.'

'Tom Coddington doesn't strike me as someone who'd be easily intimidated. Especially by a woman.'

There was silence. Benny heard the sound of a match striking, then cigarette smoke wafted inside through the open door.

'He might not be intimidated by a woman but he's quite happy to be fucked by one.'

'Frances, you have no shame.'

'Don't you get on your high horse with me, Vivienne. You were just going to let it happen, you were too lazy. Or too scared. Going to a special school would be the worst thing for Benny; he'd learn nothing except how to make beaded necklaces. He needs to be stimulated and challenged. And if that means I have to fuck the principal to make it happen, it's a small price to pay for his future.'

Benny didn't understand it at the time. He didn't know what fuck meant. But recalling the conversation in later years, he realised what had happened. After that, every time he saw Mr Coddington all he could think of was him and Auntie Fran together naked, and his cheeks would go red and he'd hang his head.

His face felt warm now just thinking of it. 'This is my stop,' the girl said.

'It's mine, too,' Benny said, though it wasn't. His stop was another few blocks away, but if he got off now he could help her. He lifted the stroller out of the luggage rack, carried it off the bus and set it up on the pavement. The girl wrestled the toddler, squirming and squealing, into the stroller and strapped her in. Benny waved to the child who immediately started gurgling and grinning.

'Thanks so much,' the girl said. Benny watched her as she walked away, pushing the stroller. She was very young, her figure still boyish, with long legs, bum-hugging shorts and a tiny tank top. Was she married? He hadn't seen a wedding ring on her finger. Maybe he should have plucked up the courage to ask her out for a date. He wouldn't mind going out with a girl who already had a child. In some ways it could be an advantage having a ready-made family. He wouldn't have to go through all the messy pregnancy and childbirth stuff.

She turned the corner. He'd missed his chance. There'd be others. Other girls, other chances. That's what Auntie Fran had said. 'Never give up, Benny,' she said, not long before she died. 'One day you'll find a girl who'll love you for who you are. And it will be worth the wait.'

He hadn't found her yet. How much longer did he have to wait?

CHAPTER 2

'Hi Mum,' Benny called as he walked in the front door, panting and sweating from his long walk in the afternoon heat.

He went over to the photo on the mantelpiece, next to the plain wooden box with the words 'Linda May Goodchild' inscribed on it. The girl in the photo was young, as young as the girl on the bus, but curvier, in a mini-skirt and low cut top, light brown curls tumbling to her shoulders. She was standing on a sand dune, the ocean in the background, head tilted and smiling at the camera as if it were her best friend. She looked like a model out of a magazine. He picked up the photo and kissed it.

'Did you have a good day?'

Of course, he knew she didn't have a good day. She was a pile of ashes in the box beside the photo. At least her body was. Even though he had no memory of her as he was only three when she died, he knew her soul was here watching over him, that she was a good mother and loved him, despite what Auntie Rose had said.

'Yeah, I had a good day,' Benny said in answer to her imagined question. 'I visited my friend Joshua this morning, and this afternoon I helped a girl on the bus with her baby.'

He felt bad lying about Joshua being his friend, but he didn't think Mum would approve of his breaking into houses. But perhaps it wasn't so bad lying to your mother when she was dead.

Benny was slurping his dinner of two minute noodles (which he'd accidentally cooked for five minutes so they were soggy), when his mobile phone buzzed with a text message. His heart sank. There was only one person who sent him text messages.

Sure enough, it was Leila, his landlady from upstairs. 'Hi Benny. Can you come up and fix my lightbulb? Thanks love.'

He couldn't ignore her; he'd tried that, and she just came down the internal staircase and banged on the door until he opened it. He texted back, 'OK. Soon.'

He finished his noodles while watching his second favourite Errol Flynn movie Captain Blood, then pressed the pause button on the DVD player remote control.

He opened the door to the internal staircase and trudged up the stairs. If only it was just to change her lightbulb. He started night shift in two hours; he'd tell Leila he was too tired.

'Come on in, honey,' she said. The incense was almost stifling. She ushered him into the living room, decorated with colourful rugs, batik wall hangings and jewelled lamps.

In the middle of the ceiling was a bare light, with the lightbulb on the table underneath it. In the background on the stereo a man was singing about a star man. Benny had heard the song before, but couldn't remember who sang it.

'I've tried and tried but the bulb just won't go in,' Leila said. Her silver-blonde hair stuck up at all angles. It was still growing back after she'd finished her chemo treatment. Her nipples were visible under her satin housecoat.

Benny focused his attention on the light. He picked up the bulb, inserted it into the socket and screwed it around clockwise. It fitted in perfectly.

Leila sighed with admiration. 'You've got the magic touch, it never works for me. Would you like a cup of tea?'

Benny shook his head.

'Something stronger—a glass of wine or champagne?' There was a half full glass of champagne on the kitchen bench.

'No, thank you.' She always asked him if he wanted a drink, even though she knew he didn't drink alcohol. He didn't like the taste of it, much preferred soft drink. 'I'm very tired and I have to go to work soon.'

Leila pouted, making her look like a fish in a fishbowl. A fish with red lipstick. 'You have to let me thank you, honey.'

She reached out and ran her fingers down his cheek. With her other hand she began to undo the buttons on his shirt, slipping her hand inside his shirt after each button and stroking his chest. Benny shivered, even though he desperately didn't want to. It happened every time; he didn't want to give in but his body had other ideas.

'I haven't been well - the chemo is still affecting me. Being with you always makes me feel so much better. '

She gave him one of her pleading looks. She overdid the eyeliner, but it didn't distract you from all the wrinkles under her eyes. Benny always felt a pang in his stomach when she mentioned her cancer, and to make matters worse, she had that illness that made you afraid of going outside. It was why he found it so difficult to refuse her. He'd watched Auntie Fran go through the chemo for her breast cancer; the days spent in bed living on water and dry crackers, her beautiful face grey and drawn, moaning that the treatment was worse than the disease.

Leila's hand slid down his stomach and with expert fingers she unzipped his jeans and pulled them and his underpants down into a puddle at his feet. She led him by his erect penis into the bedroom. A candle burned on the table next to the four poster bed, its lacy canopy curtained off to the side. Leila threw off her robe and stood naked in front of him.

'Touch me Benny, I'm all yours.'

Benny ran his hands over her body. If he closed his eyes and tried really hard, he could imagine that Leila was Auntie Fran. She had the same intense blue eyes and husky voice as Auntie Fran, but that was where the resemblance ended.

Leila was all scrawny muscle, in keeping with her previous career as an actress and dancer. Auntie Fran was much softer and more curvaceous. Not that he'd had sex with Auntie Fran; only in his imagination. Of course it was wrong to have feelings like that for your auntie, but that just made it more exciting. And it meant that he suffered twice as much guilt every time he and Leila had sex. Guilt for wishing that Leila was Auntie Fran, and thinking of

Auntie Fran when he was having sex. Besides the fact that she was related to him, she was dead. It didn't seem right, but he couldn't help himself.

He and Leila were lying on the bed facing each other, limbs entwined, her rock hard nipples pressing into his chest. He had to admit, she had good boobs for an older lady; she made no secret of her breast and lip enhancements.

'Let's take this nice and slowly,' Leila breathed. 'I've been listening to Bowie and I'm feeling in a melancholy mood.'

Leila made love according to the mood of whichever artist she'd been listening to, which she claimed was a habit from her method acting days, though Benny had no idea what method acting was. If it was the Rolling Stones, it was fast and furious, if it was the Carpenters, it was soft and dreamy. Could he persuade Leila to listen to some hymns? Perhaps something religious would put her off thoughts of sex altogether.

'I dated Bowie for a while,' she said, as she took his hand and placed it in between her legs. 'It was while I was playing the lead in Cabaret in the West End in London. He is quite the gentleman you know, a lovely soft man…not so fast, just a little slower.'

'We can't be too slow,' Benny said. 'I'll get into trouble if I'm late for work. '

'We have plenty of time,' Leila said. 'Just keep doing that right there, that's wonderful.'

Afterwards, as they lay damp and panting in each other's arms, Benny looked at the bedside clock. 9.30. Shit, he only had 30 minutes to shower, dress and get to work. He disentangled himself from Leila. 'I have to go.'

He went into the living room, picked up his clothes from the floor and got dressed. The more he tried to hurry, the more his fingers fumbled. Leila's voice floated out from the bedroom. 'Come in and give me a goodbye kiss.'

Benny went in and as he leaned over, she pulled his face down and gave him a passionate kiss. 'Thank you, darling.'

He looked down at her sprawled naked on the bed. 'Did you really date David Bowie?'

'Of course I did, I wouldn't lie to you.'

According to Leila, she'd been good friends and/or slept with just about every well-known actor and rock star from the 1970s and 80s.

'It was in his Ziggy Stardust phase. He told me I was his muse. I'd like to think that in some way I contributed to the album. Would you mind bringing in my champagne before you go?'

CHAPTER 3

The mid-summer night warmth was stifling as Benny raced along the suburban streets on his push-bike. So much for Leila saying they had plenty of time. The truth was that although he had sex with her because he was sorry for her, she also made him feel good about himself.

She liked his body and thought he was sexy; even Shona, the only proper girlfriend he'd ever had, had never told him that. And when Benny looked at himself in the mirror, at his already thinning hair, flabby belly and big feet, he didn't think he was in the least bit sexy. Not like Errol Flynn or Clint Eastwood or John Wayne.

Leila had even met Clint Eastwood one night at a party and said that he, Benny was sexier. He didn't believe her at first, but she was insistent. Now, whenever he saw Clint Eastwood on TV he got a funny buzzy feeling in the stomach, remembering what Leila had said.

The two big warehouses of Lotus Flower Imports and Exports loomed ahead. Benny checked his watch. 10.00 p.m. Hopefully Ned would be holed up in his office reading his girlie magazines, and not notice that Benny was late.

He parked his bike in the bike rack and padlocked it. As he punched his code into the time-clock, Ned lumbered out of his office, wiping crumbs from his beard, the huge cliff of his belly hanging over his pants.

'Late again bad boy,' Ned said. 'One more time and you'll have your pay docked.'

'Yes, sir,' Benny mumbled and scooted away to the far end of the warehouse where his forklift was waiting.

He passed Travis and Mick loading boxes into the back of a van. Mick ignored him as he usually did. Travis waved. 'Hey, bad boy!'

Benny didn't wave back. He hated being called bad boy. Travis thought he was so funny, coming up with that nickname because of his surname being Goodchild. But he'd been called bad boy all his life, from his first days of school.

Ned ambled over to Benny and pointed to several stacks of boxes at the far end of the warehouse. 'They all need to be shifted to the front room for transportation, so get your arse moving.'

Benny got into the forklift, started up and drove in the direction of the boxes. His spirits lifted. He loved being in charge of his own vehicle, moving loads up and down and in and out of trucks. It was all about timing and knowing which levers to use. His case officer at disability employment services had helped him to get his licence, and it was the best thing he'd ever done. While he was in the forklift he didn't have to listen to Travis and Mick cracking jokes that he didn't understand and trying to drag him into their conversations.

On the side of the boxes was stamped 'Ceramics.' He had to be extra careful with the boxes because a lot of them contained breakable goods. Lotus Flower imported a variety of goods from furniture down to small knickknacks from various Asian countries, and distributed them to a chain of stores throughout the country.

None of the goods appealed to Benny. They reminded him of things that he saw in Leila's house—incense holders in the shape of elephants, brocaded cushions and tasselled lamps. The sorts of things Auntie Rose used to call cheap Asian shit. Auntie Fran said Auntie Rose was up herself.

The shrill tea break whistle sounded through Benny's ear muffs. He'd been in such a hurry to get to work he'd forgotten to pack himself a snack. Instead of heading off to the tea room with the others, he sat at the doorway and looked up at the stars sprinkled all over the sky. A light breeze cooled his perspiration. The man on the weather report had said they were having the hottest summer on record.

It was peaceful here; he didn't like being with the others at tea break. They always talked about things he wasn't interested in; cars, football and drinking. And the way they talked about women was disgraceful. As if they were just objects to be used and thrown away. Once Mick boasted about being involved in a gang bang, and Benny was so sick in the stomach he had to get up and leave. He wished he had the courage to tell them what he thought.

'Hey bad boy, are you coming?'

Travis was walking towards him. Benny shook his head.

'You okay?' Travis said. 'Where's your tucker?'

'I forgot to pack it.'

'Have some of mine.'

Travis sat down beside him, opened a paper bag and took out a sandwich. He handed Benny one half of it. 'Here, get your choppers around this one. My missus makes a mean sandwich.'

Benny took a bite. Travis was right, it was delicious. Lashings of ham, cheese and tomato on soft, white bread. As he ate, he felt Travis watching him. On the surface Travis was friendly enough, but he often made Benny feel uncomfortable. Now he was looking at Benny with a strange expression, as if he were a puzzle and Travis was trying to work him out.

'How long have you been working here now?' Travis asked.

'I think…' Benny paused to work it out. 'About two years.'

'Good on ya, that's longer than I've ever stayed in a job. Do you like it?'

Benny shrugged. 'It's okay.'

'The pay's pretty shit, though, isn't it?'

Benny had never thought about whether the pay was good or not. After he paid his rent and bought his groceries and put aside some money for his phone and electricity, he had just enough left for the occasional apple cream tart from the bakery and a DVD from Fishpond to add to his steadily growing collection.

Travis leaned closer to Benny and said in a low voice, 'How would you like to earn yourself some extra cash?'

'How?'

'Helping Mick and me in a little business venture,' Travis said.

'What sort of business venture?'

'Let's just say that Mick and I have a little import business of our own.'

'Importing what?'

'You have to agree to it first,' Travis said, 'because if I tell you, and you don't agree to it, I'll have to kill you.'

Benny gaped at him. Travis grinned and slapped him on the shoulder. 'Just joking. About killing you, anyway.'

'So it must be illegal,' Benny said.

'Brilliant deduction bad boy, who said you were slow?'

Travis looked around him, saw there was no one in the vicinity, and dragged a packet of cigarettes out of his pants pocket. He slipped one out and lit it up, blowing the smoke into the night air. 'Okay, I'll tell you anyway. Mick and I will be unloading some goods from certain boxes that come in. We need you to be a lookout in case Ned decides to come and stick his big nose into what we're doing.'

Benny pointed to the nearest security camera looking down at them from the ceiling. 'He'll see you anyhow, there are cameras everywhere.'

'Not everywhere, mate. There are a couple of blind spots we've sussed out.'

'How much do I get?' Benny asked.

'Depends on the size of the load; could be anywhere up to five thousand.'

'Five thousand dollars,' Benny said, 'for being a lookout.'

It was a lot of money—he couldn't believe that Travis would pay him so much for doing nothing except watching out for Ned. But Travis must have thought that he meant it the other way, that it wasn't enough, because he frowned and said, 'You're only a beginner, mate. See how you go on the first job and we might give you a raise.'

He stubbed his cigarette out on the concrete and threw it into the bushes. 'Are you in?'

Benny shook his head. 'I don't want to do anything that's against the law.'

'Is that a fact?' Travis said, 'You're not living up to your name, bad boy. Never mind, your loss.'

As he got up he said in Benny's ear, 'And if you tell anybody about this, it's only your word against mine and no one will believe a simpleton like you.

And then I'll punch you so hard you won't be able to stand up for a week.'

The whistle blew for the end of tea break. Travis got up and sauntered inside.

#

Back on the forklift, Benny thought about Travis's offer. It had to be drugs. The last thing he wanted was to get himself in trouble. After the magistrate threatened to send him to jail if he re-offended, he decided to become smarter about the way he did things and learned how to pick locks. It was that combined with pure luck that had got him this far without any further run-ins with the police. But he didn't want to push his luck by getting involved with drugs.

He hoped that Travis wouldn't be too annoyed with him for turning down his offer, and make his life more difficult than usual. At 7.00 a.m. the whistle blew. Benny parked the forklift, ready for the morning shift to take over. He swiped his card to knock off, jumped on his bike and pedalled out the front gate.

As he rode along the streets the sun was already a brilliant ball in the sky. He enjoyed watching the suburb coming alive. People walking their dogs, the early morning workers hurrying to the bus or train station, the huge trucks grumbling their way towards the industrial precinct he'd just left. It felt good coming home from work just as everyone else was starting their day.

As he rounded the corner into the more residential part of Marrickville, two blocks from home, he saw a removal van parked on the street in front of a small house. Two men, broad-shouldered and tattooed in singlets and shorts, were carrying a leather couch through the front gate.

Benny was about to veer into the middle of the road to avoid the truck when he spied a woman standing at the front door. Slim, shoulder-length blonde hair, in tights and a T-shirt. As the men came towards her, she stepped outside to let them through.

As Benny came closer he saw her face clearly. Heart-shaped, dainty nose, full lips. As perfect as a sculpture. He couldn't take his eyes off her; she was the most beautiful woman he had ever seen.

The next thing he knew he was heading straight for the truck. He swerved just in time and wobbled onto the footpath. The bike crashed and flung Benny onto the pavement.

He heard the slam of a gate and then Benny found himself looking at a pair of pink joggers. 'Are you all right?' said a soft, female voice.

Benny pushed himself up from the ground. 'Yes,' he mumbled.

'Look at your hands! Come inside and let me bathe them for you.'

Benny studied his hands. His palms were grazed and his knees were stinging inside his jeans.

He looked up at her. Her eyes, blue-green like the ocean, shone with concern.

'I'm okay,' he said. 'I live around the corner; I can wash them at home.'

'Well, if you're sure,' she said. 'Is your bike okay?'

Benny picked up his bike and looked over it. It had suffered a couple of dents but no major damage. 'It's fine.'

The two removalists came out of the house and looked at Benny. 'Didn't you see the truck, mate?' one of them said and they both guffawed.

'Thank-you anyway,' Benny said to the woman. He mounted his bike and rode off.

#

Benny plonked himself down on the couch with the plate of rubbery scrambled eggs he'd cooked himself for breakfast. The accident played itself over and over in his head like a video on an endless loop. What an idiot he was for falling off his bike in front of the most beautiful woman in the world. But she had caused it; he was so enchanted by this vision from a Walt Disney movie. And she was just as beautiful on the inside, so kind and caring, offering to bathe his cuts. He would have taken up her offer, just to have a few minutes in her company, if he wasn't so embarrassed.

Thinking about her now, his heart thumped like a jackhammer and he felt light in the head. He'd heard of love at first sight. Was this it? He'd never been in love, not even with Shona, which he hoped might be love, but turned out to be the exact opposite. He'd rescued her from the streets, walked past her as she was begging for money and feeling sorry for her, offered her a bed for a couple of nights.

A couple of nights turned into six months. She shared his bed and for a while, it was nice. Nice to have someone to cuddle up to, to wake up and have breakfast with. He didn't know what she did while he was at work—back then, he worked days in a biscuit factory—but after a few weeks she started staying out all night, and then turning up the next day as if nothing had happened.

When Benny asked her where she'd been, she snapped, 'None of your business, you don't own me.' And she stopped wanting to have sex. By the time Benny had decided to ask her to leave, she'd packed all her stuff into his favourite overnight bag, the one Auntie Fran had given him, and had run off to live with another man. But what he'd felt for Shona after six months was nothing like he felt for this woman, whom he'd met for only a few minutes and whose name he didn't even know.

Usually after breakfast Benny would watch some TV or put on a DVD to help him wind down before going to bed. He never slept for more than four or five hours, and was up again by lunchtime. But this time he was too wound up, couldn't even begin to think of sleeping. He cleaned his flat from top to bottom, which didn't take very long because it was only three rooms—a combined kitchen and living room, and a tiny bedroom and bathroom. Then he rearranged his collection of Disney cartoon characters on the window sill so they were all in straight lines horizontally and vertically.

Finally, at 11.00 a.m. he fell into bed, exhausted.

CHAPTER 4

'Hey, bad boy! Watch what you're doing!'

Benny jumped, and noticed he had almost driven the forklift into the back wall of the warehouse. Then Ned was beside him, belly quivering. 'You've been in a trance all night. Keep your mind on the job.'

'Sorry,' Benny mumbled. He forced his mind away from visions of his blonde princess to the pile of boxes he was moving to be loaded onto the truck. Was it only a day since he'd seen her? It seemed like a lifetime; before he met her was his old life; now this was his bright new life.

As he rode his bike home after work, he slowed down approaching her house, hoping by some miracle she might be outside. But she wasn't. The shutters on the windows were closed and the house was still and silent. Was she still in bed? She probably had a job; maybe she'd left for work already. If not, maybe he could still catch a glimpse of her.

Benny whizzed around the corner, dropped his push-bike at home and walked back to her street again. There was a bus stop a few houses along; if he sat there he could see her when she came out the front gate. He sat and waited. An old woman with a shopping trolley waddled over and parked herself on the seat next to him.

'It's going to be another hot one,' she said.

'Yes,' Benny agreed. He stared fixedly in the opposite direction, willing the blonde woman to arrive. If he closed his eyes and wished really hard.

He opened his eyes. It was no good her turning up here if he was sitting here like an idiot with his eyes closed. He looked down the road and spied a figure walking towards him. Slim, female, blonde. His heart started thumping crazily. It was her!

She was dressed in a skirt, jacket and high heels and her hair was up in a ponytail. As she came nearer, he heard a phone ring tone. She pulled a phone out of her handbag and started speaking.

'The real estate agent gave me your name,' he heard her say, as she stopped beside the bus stop. She hadn't seen him yet. What was he going to say? He would have to pretend he was taking the bus.

'You really can't help me?' she said. 'I just moved in, but the yard's a mess. I need someone to mow my lawn and do a bit of gardening once a fortnight. It wouldn't take more than an hour.'

She listened, then said, 'Can you recommend anyone else?'

Another pause, then, 'Okay, I'll try them. Thank you.'

She slipped her phone back into her handbag, looked around and saw Benny.

She smiled. It lit up her face and made her look like an angel. Like those angels in the paintings in the art gallery Auntie Rose had taken him to when he lived with her.

'Hello. Have you recovered from yesterday?'

Benny opened his hands and looked at the grazes, which he'd bathed and doused in antiseptic cream, as well as the ones on his knees. It had only hurt a bit.

'I'm okay.'

'That's good. Are you taking the bus today instead of riding your bike?'

Benny nodded. His tongue felt as if it were tied in knots. Why couldn't he say something witty like Errol Flynn? Her perfume wafted over; it made him heady.

'I can mow your lawn for you,' he blurted out.

She looked at him, surprised.

His face warmed. 'I'm sorry, I heard you talking on your phone. I didn't mean to be rude.'

'That's okay. Do you have a lawn mowing business?'

'No, but I can mow a lawn. I do it for my landlady.'

She had that look on her face that people get when they are going to say no, and they're trying to work out how to do it without hurting your feelings.

'I know how to do gardening too,' he said. He wasn't at all sure he could; he used to help Auntie Vi with her gardening and often pulled up more flowers than weeds. But Auntie Fran always said, 'Fake it until you make it. If you pretend you can do it, you're half way there.'

'And I'll do it for free,' he added.

The woman was studying him, then gave him another one of her smiles. 'That's very nice of you. All right, I'll give you a go. When can you start?'

'Whenever you want.'

'How about Saturday morning at 8 o'clock?'

Benny nodded.

'I don't own a lawn mower,' she said.

'That's okay, I can borrow my landlady's.'

A bus appeared at the top of the street. 'Here's my bus. Is this yours, too?'

'No,' Benny said. 'I'm going…somewhere else.'

'I guess we'd better introduce ourselves. I'm Olivia.'

Olivia. Like Olivia de Havilland. When Benny first saw her as Maid Marion in The Adventures of Robin Hood he thought she was the most stunning creature he'd ever seen. And this Olivia was just as stunning—even more so, because she was young, and Olivia de Havilland would be very old now. If only he could be as handsome and full of confidence as Errol Flynn.

'I'm Benny.'

As the bus pulled up, she said, 'See you on Saturday, Benny. You know where I live.'

He watched her as she stepped on to the bus and sat on a window seat. Her hair glinted in the sun shining through the window and her soft, sweet voice echoed in his head. The bus lurched forward and rumbled away.

#

Olivia's house was tiny, more like a cottage, painted a cheerful yellow with blue trim. It made Benny happy just looking at it.

He opened the front gate and walked in. The trick was to always walk in as if you owned the place, as if you were meant to be there. With Olivia having only moved in three days ago, any nosy neighbours were not to know that he wasn't also living there.

He did a quick tour of the cottage looking for open windows. There were none, and they all had security screens on them. He was glad for her sake; you never knew what strange people were lurking around.

He went around to the back door. Just outside was a small outdoor table and two chairs, overlooking a small backyard and a flower garden that ran the length of the back fence.

He peered in through the window. Through the partially open shutters he could see a small laundry. In the corner was a large pile of flattened cardboard boxes. The door was locked. He examined the lock—it was a standard pin and tumbler lock common to many modern homes.

He dug into his jeans pocket and drew out his tools of trade—a tension wrench and a hairpin. Much as some people were amazingly careless about their home security, you could never count on it. Like now. He was inside within 30 seconds. Possibly a personal best.

If only Travis and Mick could see him now; they wouldn't think he was so stupid. He'd taught himself to pick locks by visiting different hardware shops, buying every type of lock he could find, and practising picking them until he was an expert at all of them.

The laundry led into the kitchen—small, but bright and modern. In the living room was the leather couch he'd seen the men carrying in, a light beige colour that blended in with the polished floorboards and the cream walls. At the end of the couch was a recliner, with a couple of cushions on it, arranged as if someone had been sitting there.

He sank into it and pulled out the handle to make the footrest come up. This must be where she sat to watch TV. Her bottom would have sat right on this very spot where his was now. It made him feel funny in the stomach. He thought he could detect a faint trace of her perfume, so he breathed in deeply to take in as much of it as he could.

He picked up the remote control from the coffee table next to him and switched on the large flat screen TV on the wall. He scrolled through the options. She didn't have pay TV; only Netflix and Stan, and as he didn't know her password, he couldn't access it. He could forgive her for that, as there were too many other interesting things in the house to look at. Because they belonged to her.

He put the footstool down, heaved himself out of the recliner and wandered into the first bedroom. A neatly made bed with a pink and brown cover and pillows and in pride of place a huge teddy bear with a red bow around its neck and a stern expression, as if it were on guard duty.

Benny looked at the two framed photos on the bedside table. One of Olivia in a gown and hat, the kind they wore at university, an older grey-blonde woman and a balding man with a moustache on either side of her. Olivia's parents; her mother was a wrinklier version of her. So Olivia was smart; she'd gone to university. No wonder the pride shone on their faces.

The other photo was of a young boy and girl standing on a beach beside a man and woman. The man and woman were a younger version of those in the other photograph, the girl and boy presumably Olivia and her brother. He studied Olivia. She looked about 9 or 10—slim and leggy, hair in pigtails, smiling shyly at the camera. Even then she looked like an angel; pure and sweet.

Benny peered into the walk-in wardrobe. The hanging space was crammed, on the floor were three racks of neatly stacked shoes. The shelves were all occupied; there were a lot of gym clothes. On the bottom shelf were neat piles of underwear; black lace peeked out from one of them. Benny looked away. He wasn't going to look at her underwear; that would be creepy.

He moved the teddy bear and stretched himself out on the bed. Through the window white clouds sailed along the blue sky, like boats on the sea. He imagined it was night, the sky dark with just a sliver of moon shining through. Olivia was snuggled up beside him under the sheets, her head on his chest, her soft body pressed against his.

His arousal embarrassed him, even though there was no one else there to witness it. He was getting ahead of himself, he'd only met her twice. But now that he was going to be her gardener, he could get to know her better. He got off the bed, straightened the cover and placed the teddy back in its position.

Was that a disapproving look in its black-button eyes?

Benny went into the bathroom. A fluffy towel hung on the towel rack and in the shower were bottles of shampoo, conditioner and peppermint body wash. He picked up the body wash, opened the bottle and sniffed. It smelt good enough to eat. On the bathroom sink lay a hairbrush packed with strands of blonde hair. He pulled out some of the strands and put them up to his nose. They smelled of cinnamon and apple. He stuffed them into his pocket.

He studied the row of tubes lined up on the basin. Apple pie cleanser, toner and moisturiser. Rose clay mask, mud and seaweed exfoliation. There weren't nearly as many as Auntie Rose used to have in her bathroom; her sink was crammed with them. She wouldn't even go to the letter box unless she had her 'face on' as she called it. But Olivia didn't need any of that stuff, she was beautiful just the way God had made her. Perhaps one day he would tell her that.

He peered into the other bedroom, which contained a desk and a pile of boxes that wasn't unpacked yet. Nothing interesting there—until she finished unpacking.

He returned to the kitchen and opened the refrigerator. Perhaps she hadn't had time to go shopping since moving in—all it contained was a bag of apples, a carton of almond milk, a take-away container of food that was mostly vegetables and an open block of 85% dark chocolate. What bad luck—he didn't like 85% chocolate; it was too bitter.

He laughed out loud when the thought struck him—this was like the story of Goldilocks and the three bears, but back to front. First, he'd tried Olivia's chair, then her bed; now he was looking for something to eat. Preferably not porridge.

He picked up a couple of leaflets from the bench. A take-away menu for an Indian restaurant and a pamphlet for the Serenity Yoga School. His Auntie Rose had loved yoga and dragged him to one of her classes. It was one of the most embarrassing times of his life. There was the downward dog, the camel, the swan, the eagle. The poses didn't resemble any of the animals they were named after and he found them all difficult. And being surrounded by slim, graceful young women (and some older ones like Auntie Rose) who could twist themselves into all sorts of positions made him feel even more awkward and clumsy. But he could easily imagine Olivia at a yoga lesson; she would outshine all the others.

He opened all the kitchen cupboards and looked inside. Plain white crockery, two stick blenders, a bright pink toaster, an electric frying pan, a vegetable steamer, a coffee percolator. Everything was stacked neatly, the plastics stored inside each other. Not like some people's cupboards, where everything burst on to the floor as soon as you opened the doors.

In the cupboard beside the sink was a straw basket. It contained odds and ends—a couple of batteries, a tiny screwdriver, a ball of string, a couple of light bulbs, a bunch of empty key rings. A pile of business cards. 'Olivia Bartlett. Hedges Real Estate. Marketing Coordinator.'

He looked at the word again. Marketing Coordinator. He couldn't even say it, but it sounded impressive. Something a smart, beautiful woman would do. He took a card and slipped it into his pocket.

At the bottom of the basket was a set of keys. The key ring was labelled 'spare keys.' Benny took the keys and tried them out on the front door. One of them unlocked the screen door and one the front door. Brilliant. He slipped out the front door, locking it as he went. An hour and a half later, he was back.

With the set of keys he'd had made up at the local hardware store, he unlocked the front door and went in. He put the bunch of spare keys back in the basket and placed it back in the cupboard. His stomach was rumbling; time to leave. Now that he had his own key, he could come back at any time while she was at work.

CHAPTER 5

At five minutes to eight on Saturday morning, Benny was ringing Olivia's front doorbell. After arriving home from work he only just had time to have a shower, douse himself in deodorant and change his clothes. He would get hot and sweaty doing the lawn, but at least he could turn up there clean.

But by the time he arrived at Olivia's house the sweat was pouring off him—the day was already steaming and he'd pushed Leila's lawn mower, a heavy old Victa, all the way along the footpath. The front door opened and Olivia stood there in a pair of gym pants and T-shirt. Her feet were bare. Benny couldn't help staring at them; they were small and narrow, perfectly formed, her toenails gleaming in pale pink.

'Hullo, Benny. How are you?'

Benny lifted his gaze. 'Good, thank you.'

'Just as well you came early, it's going to be very hot today.'

'Yes, it is.'

She nodded at the lawn mower. 'Bring it around to the back yard and I'll show you what to do.'

She disappeared inside. He pushed the lawn mower around the side of the house to the back, where she met him at the back door.

The small lawn was straggly and overgrown. He hadn't taken much notice of it when he broke into her house. She motioned him over to the garden at the back fence. In between patches of brightly coloured flowers were clumps of weeds, some of them higher than the flowers.

'If you could weed this garden as well, that would be great. The tenant before me just let it grow wild. If it were up to me, I'd pull all the flowers out and put in a veggie garden.'

'The flowers are pretty, though,' Benny said.

Olivia smiled. 'Yes, they are. But no one can see them, and I don't have time to sit out here and admire them. Knock on the back door when you're finished.'

He watched her as she disappeared again into the house. He'd filled the mower with petrol before he left home, but because it was old and sluggish it took several attempts to start it. He had to go over the lawn a couple of times to catch all the grass, which almost filled the grass catcher.

He took a handkerchief out of his pocket, wiped the sweat from his face, then started on the garden. He was bending over at first, then he remembered what Auntie Vi told him. 'It's bad for your back, you should kneel.'

He kneeled, but it became uncomfortable after a while. Auntie Vi had used a special embroidered kneeling mat. And gardening gloves. It was difficult to grab the weeds with his bare hands as they were slippery. But he pulled up as many as he could, resulting in two large piles of weeds. From them peeked splashes of colour, where he'd accidentally pulled out a flower.

He picked out all the flowers into their own pile, looked around to make sure Olivia wasn't watching, and threw it over the fence, into the yard of the cottage behind him. He picked up the weeds and placed them in the garbage bin at the side of the house. Then wiping his hands on his shorts, he approached the back door and knocked.

Olivia opened the door, came out and inspected the lawn and the garden. 'You did a great job, Benny. That looks so much tidier. Would you like a drink?'

'Yes, please.'

He'd been hoping she'd offer him a drink; anything to prolong the time he spent with her. He sat down at the outdoor table. She went inside and re-appeared with a tall glass of orange juice on ice. She placed it on the table and was just about to sit down in the other chair when a mobile phone started ringing. 'Excuse me,' she said and went back inside.

Benny slurped his juice and surveyed the lawn and garden. It certainly looked a lot neater, but not for long, he hoped. The sooner the grass and weeds grew back, the sooner she would have a reason to ask him back.

'No, I can't Lucas, I have something else on tonight.' Olivia's voice floated out through the open back door. Her voice was raised a little; she sounded annoyed. 'I'm not going to explain, you know why.'

She re-appeared, sat down and poured herself a juice. 'Are you admiring your handiwork?' she asked.

'I'm admiring the flowers. You said you didn't have time to sit and admire them and I felt sorry for them.'

Olivia laughed. 'All right, I'll make a point of coming outside every day and admiring them.'

He felt her looking sideways at him. 'So Benny, do you have a job?'

'Yes.' He told her about the job at Lotus Flower.

'Do you like it?'

'It's okay. Some of the other workers are a bit mean but I'm used to it.'

'How are they mean?'

'They call me names, make jokes about me and hide my push-bike. Once they hid my dinner and my push-bike on the same night.'

Olivia looked at him with disbelief. 'And these are grown men? How ridiculous!'

'When I first started they took me to the pub one night and put vodka in my orange juice. I didn't know, and I got really drunk and I was dancing, and they laughed at me and then I got sick and vomited all over the floor. Then they got really mad at me and left me there, and the manager of the pub had to clean me up and call a taxi for me.'

Olivia was staring at him, open-mouthed. 'What pigs! Why are you still working there?'

'Ned had a talk to them, and they were nicer to me after that.'

Sort of. They still made fun of him when Ned wasn't around to hear them, but at least they'd stopped playing tricks on him.

'I hope they are,' Olivia said.

Benny slurped some more of his juice, then remembering his manners, sipped at the rest.

Olivia looked at her watch. 'I'm sorry to rush you, but I've got a class to go to shortly.'

'Is it yoga?' As soon as he opened his mouth, Benny realised his mistake. Olivia gave him a strange look. 'Yes. How did you know?'

How was he going to get out of this? He could hardly tell her he'd seen the pamphlet on her kitchen bench. Whenever he needed to think quickly, his brain turned to mush.

'I just thought you looked like someone who would do yoga.' She continued to look at him oddly. 'Well, you look very flexible,' he blundered on, 'like you could do the downward dog and all that stuff.'

To his relief, she burst out laughing. 'The downward dog is the easy part. Have you ever done yoga?'

'A couple of times. I wasn't very good at it.'

'It takes time. Just wait there a minute.'

She went inside and returned holding some notes. She thrust them at him. 'I can't let you do this for nothing.'

Benny shook his head. 'It's okay, I don't mind.'

'Yes, but I do. It's only fair you get paid for your work. I'm sure you've had a lot of people take advantage of you, but I'm not going to be one of them.'

Benny took the notes—a twenty and a ten—and shoved them in his pocket. Maybe it wasn't so bad after all to be paid for it; he could order a few more Clint Eastwood DVDs. He'd made over 40 movies and Benny only had 25.

'Can you come every fortnight at the same time? Saturday at 8 o'clock?' Olivia asked.

Only every fortnight! Did he have to wait that long to see her again?

'Yes,' he said, trying hard not to show his disappointment.

#

At 9.00 a.m. Benny knocked on the front door of Olivia's cottage. He had to make sure she wasn't home; that she wasn't sick or taking a day off work. His heart thumped as he strained his ears for any sounds of movement inside. He had no idea what he would say if she opened the door; it had only been two days since he'd mowed her lawn.

He'd longed to go to the bus stop and wait for her, to see her again and hear her voice and talk to her. He replayed their conversation on Saturday morning over and over in his mind; she was interested in what he had to say, treated him like a normal person, and it made him feel warm inside. But she would think he was being creepy hanging around the bus stop, especially when it became obvious he wasn't catching a bus.

Silence inside. Benny slid his keys out of his pocket, unlocked the front door and slipped inside. The kitchen was immaculate; a bowl, spoon and coffee mug were draining on the sideboard. He opened the refrigerator. There was more in it than last time, but nothing that looked appetising. Goat's cheese, rye crackers, a couple of avocados and a packet of salad vegetables. And the bag of apples.

He took an apple out of the open bag; there were plenty in there so she wouldn't miss one, and settled himself on the recliner chair. Crunching into his apple, he turned the TV on to the shopping channel. A man was soaping a window with a long pole that had a sponge on the end. Inside the room, a young woman with puffy lips and a low-cut dress was talking animatedly to Benny. He knew she was really talking to the TV camera, but she was looking straight at him.

'Not only does the Ezy Window Washer have a reversible head for shiny, spotless glass'—the man turned the stick around and wiped all the water from the window—'it also has an extendable brush attachment for getting those hard to reach cobwebs.'

The man took the sponge head off and replaced it with a brush, then reached up and began to brush the ceiling, all the while grinning at Benny, as if brushing away cobwebs was the most exciting job in the world. Benny immediately wanted one, even though he never cleaned his windows or ceiling. But the reason he never did them was because he didn't have an Ezy Window Washer. If he had one, he would wash his windows and brush away the cobwebs all the time. Leila would certainly be impressed.

But the process of ringing the number on the TV screen and ordering it over the phone was a bit too scary for Benny. Which was probably lucky, because he didn't want to end up like his Auntie Vi. She had been addicted to the shopping channels and ordered everything. The house was filled to the rafters with goods that she never used, overflowing from the spare bedroom to the rest of the house, and Benny had to carve a path from the front door to his bedroom.

Later, Auntie Fran told him that Auntie Vi was depressed because she was in love with her best friend Grace, who was very la-di-da and married to a man in a high position in the local council. Auntie Vi didn't have the courage to tell Grace how she felt about her, and when Grace moved to another town far away, Auntie Vi became very sad, locked herself in her room and wouldn't eat. That was when Benny went to live with Auntie Rose. Benny felt sad every time he thought of Auntie Vi. How terrible it must be to love someone so much and not be able to tell them.

He finished his apple, put the core in his pocket to dispose of later and turned off the TV. He wandered into the second bedroom. The boxes had all been unpacked, and the desk was bare except for a lamp and a pink laptop. He opened the laptop and switched it on. A box popped up asking for the password. Bad luck. He turned off the laptop and opened the top drawer of the desk. A tray of pencils, pens and erasers. A pile of sticky notes. A stapler and a packet of paper clips.

In the second drawer was a pile of papers. He picked up the top one and unfolded it. It was a letter addressed to Ms Olivia Bartlett.

'Dear Ms Bartlett
Re: divorce proceedings.

I regret to inform you that as you and Mr Lucas Bartlett had a period of reconciliation recently, you must wait another 12 months from the date you separated before you can institute divorce proceedings.

Please let me know if I can be of any further assistance during this time.

Kind Regards
Paul Butler
Butler and Young, Solicitors.'

Benny read the letter slowly. Big words always tripped him up, but he could often work out their meaning from the other words around them. So Olivia had been married to this Lucas guy and now wanted a divorce. Lucas— wasn't that the name of the person she was speaking to on the phone when he was here on Saturday? She didn't sound very happy to hear from him. What an idiot Lucas must be, to upset a woman like Olivia. If he, Benny, were married to Olivia, he would do everything he could to make her happy.

He opened the second drawer. There were two framed photos, face down. He pulled them out and placed them on the desk. They were both wedding photos. One was of Olivia and Lucas with their attendants; two of each. Olivia looked like a princess out of a storybook in her flowing ivory gown and her hair up, with soft curls falling around her face. Lucas was tall and thin, with spiky blonde hair and a short, neat beard.

Benny studied him. He was quite good looking, except he had thin lips. Auntie Fran always said to never trust a man with thin lips. The second photo was a close-up of the two of them, side on, with a backdrop of the sea, smiling into each other's eyes. Lucas had his hand over her veil as if he had just lifted it off her face.

Benny felt a stab of pain in his heart. Would any woman ever look at him like that, as if she could see nothing else but him? He put the photos back and opened the bottom drawer.

A folder marked 'Personal Documents' was on the top. Benny opened it and looked through the documents. Birth certificate. She was born in Perth on 26 January 1983. Benny was born in 1974. He tried to calculate the difference. Maths wasn't his strong point either; nothing was his strong point. In any case, it meant she was in her thirties, a few years younger than he.

A degree from the University of Sydney, Bachelor of Arts, with majors in Communication and Marketing. A letter addressed to 'whom it may concern' saying that Ms Olivia Bartlett had worked at Pizzaz Marketing as a marketing co-ordinator for the last three years and had been diligent and innovative with excellent customer skills. Signed Brett Makerston, Director. Diligent and innovative—big words that made her sound impressive.

He dug down into the folder and drew out a passport. A couple of stamps in it; the countries weren't clear, but he thought he could make out Indonesia and New Zealand.

A marriage certificate of Olivia Joanne Southwell to Lucas Martin Bartlett at St Anthony's Uniting Church in Woollongong on 5 May 2008.

A certificate from East-West Skydiving calling her a skydiving legend. 'I jumped out of a plane and survived!' She was braver than he was; he couldn't imagine himself ever jumping out of a plane. Another two certificates—one from the Thai School of Cooking to say she'd completed a course in Hot and Spicy Thai Cooking and another from the Modern School of Languages, at which she'd achieved a high distinction in basic Italian. Was there nothing she couldn't do?

A wave of sadness swamped him. Olivia was smart, talented and beautiful. A woman like that would never want someone like him. Except in his dreams. And dreams were nice, but you couldn't hug a dream, or talk to it. Or love it.

#

It wasn't enough to hang around in her house, to breathe in the air she breathed, sit on her couch, lie on her bed, get the wedding photos out of her desk drawer and gaze at them, imagining himself in the photos instead of Lucas. After a few visits he began to feel restless. He wanted to see her in the flesh, and he couldn't wait another two days until it was time to mow her lawn again.

Thursday was his rostered night off. He had an early dinner, and as darkness began to fall he left home, ambling along the street as if he were out for an evening stroll. It was a warm night and he was hot by the time he arrived at Olivia's house. The windows were lit up, so she was home.

Benny climbed over the low front fence and crept around to the kitchen window. The window was half open and hiding in a nearby tangle of shrubs, he could see into the kitchen through the open shutters. A clattering of cooking noises floated out into the evening air. Then Olivia came into his view and his heart leapt.

She had on a pair of shorts and a midriff T-shirt that exposed her smooth belly, and she was stirring something in a saucepan on the stove. A curry-like aroma wafted out. Benny's stomach rumbled. He'd only had a ham sandwich for dinner.

The sound of a doorbell rang through the house. Olivia looked annoyed. She placed the saucepan on a cork mat on the bench and hurried out of the kitchen. She returned shortly afterwards, followed by a tall, slim man. Benny recognised him as Lucas, though his hair was longer and his beard scruffier than in the wedding photos. He strolled in with a confident air, as if he owned the place.

Olivia's face was pale as she faced him. 'How did you find out my address?'

'I have my ways.'

'It's an invasion of my privacy.'

'Bullshit, I have a right to know where my wife is living.'

'I'm not your wife,' Olivia said. 'We separated, remember?'

'Only until we can sort things out.'

Olivia shook her head. 'We've tried to sort things out and it didn't work. I want to know - how did you find me?'

Lucas shrugged. 'I followed you home from work one day.'

Olivia gasped. 'You stalked me!'

Anger flashed across Lucas's face. 'I didn't stalk you. You're my wife. How can I stalk my own wife?'

'And I've told you before, I am not your wife,' Olivia said.

Lucas's hand shot out and slapped Olivia's face with a resounding smack. She cried out and he took hold of her shoulders, pushed her up against the kitchen sink and pushed his face right up to hers. 'You are legally my wife and you can't deny that.'

Benny was shaking and had a horrible feeling in the pit of his stomach. He could hardly believe what he'd seen. He wanted to jump in through the window and smash his fist right into Lucas's face. If he were Errol Flynn he would break the door down, race in, knock Lucas out and carry Olivia out in his arms.

Then Lucas stepped back and smiled. It was a creepy smile, because of his thin lips. 'Now let's talk about this sensibly. How about we sit down and have dinner and a glass of wine and we can sort things out like two civilised human beings.'

Lucas sat at the table and watched Olivia as she got two plates out of the cupboard and scooped the contents of the saucepan on to them. She took another saucepan off the stove, emptied the water and scooped some noodles onto each dish. She placed both plates on the table, then went to the fridge and got out a bottle of wine and two wine glasses. Lucas poured them both a large glass.

When Olivia sat down at the table, she was facing Benny. He ducked down, but not before he saw her swollen red cheek. He clenched his fists. There was silence for a few moments, only broken by the clinking of cutlery on plates.

Then Lucas spoke. The table was near the window, so even crouched below it he could hear them clearly.

'I've been thinking. I've changed my mind about going to counselling. I'll come with you.'

'You've said that before.' Olivia's voice was flat. 'And if you remember at the first counselling session you shouted at the counsellor and stalked out of the room.'

'She wasn't a good counsellor, she was too biased. If we can find someone else, I promise I'll behave.'

'It's too late, Lucas,' Olivia said.

'I love you, Olivia, I will love you until the day I die. Remember our vows - till death us do part.'

'I'm sorry Lucas, I don't love you anymore.'

There was a loud thud, like someone thumping their fist on the table. 'That's bullshit! I know you love me, otherwise you wouldn't have agreed to a reconciliation six months ago. The separation is just another one of your pigheaded ideas.'

There was a loud sound of something crashing and breaking, then footsteps strode out. A door banged shut. Then silence. Benny popped his head up and cautiously peered through the window.

Olivia was slumped forward at the table. Her head was on her hands and her shoulders were shaking, but there was no sound. Benny shifted a little and twisted his head around to get a better view of the kitchen. A mess of food was dripping down the cupboard door under the sink, to a pile of broken crockery on the floor.

A car door slammed, an engine started and roared down the street. Benny stood for a while, watching Olivia. All sorts of feelings were whirling around inside him, mixed together like a stew so he didn't know what he felt—anger, sadness, love. And helplessness. There was nothing he could do right at this moment to help Olivia, to make her feel better.

He eased himself out of the shrubbery, crept out of the yard and made his way home.

CHAPTER 6

Lucas had his hands around Olivia's throat. She was going blue in the face and her eyes were just about popping out of her head. Lucas was yelling at her as his hands squeezed tighter around her throat.

Bennie burst in through the window with a gun. He pointed it at Lucas.

'Let go of her now!'

Lucas snarled and before Benny's eyes morphed into a huge dragon, breathing fire. He picked up Olivia, put her on his back and flew out the window. There was a loud incessant chiming. Was that someone at the front door? Bennie would have to go and tell them that Olivia was no longer there, that he'd failed to save her from Lucas and that Lucas would kill her.

The chiming continued and Bennie opened his eyes in a lather of sweat. The chiming sound was his phone. He picked it up and blearily pressed the answer button without looking at the caller ID.

'Hello honey,' Leila said. 'Can you come up and help an old lady open a can of tomatoes? My old pal Arthur Itis is giving me hell today.'

Leila never mentioned Arthur Itis unless she wanted him to do something for her. And it never seemed to interfere with her enjoyment of sex. Benny sighed to himself and looked at his watch.

Four-twenty. He'd slept longer than he'd intended, but he still had that tired, dragging feeling. He'd gone straight from work to mowing Olivia's lawn. She had to go out as soon as he was finished, so they didn't exchange more than a few words.

After returning home and a late breakfast, he'd started watching Rio

Bravo, one of his favourite John Wayne movies, on the DVD player. The last thing he remembered was the scene where John Wayne picked up a sleeping Angie Dickinson in his arms and took her upstairs. Benny was picturing himself as John Wayne and Olivia as Angie Dickinson and then he must have fallen asleep on the couch.

'I'm making spaghetti bolognese for dinner,' Leila purred. 'You're welcome to stay and have some.'

It was his favourite dish, and Leila knew it. Could he eat it and then make some excuse to come straight home? Leila always seemed to know when he was making excuses. But spaghetti bolognese...

'I've got garlic bread as well,' Leila said.

'Okay,' Benny said. 'I'll be there in a few minutes.'

He splashed cold water on his face to wake himself up, then went up the internal stairs and knocked on the door. It opened and Leila stood there in a thin, flowing dress.

He followed her into the kitchen, and with the light shining on her he could see she was wearing nothing underneath. He swallowed hard and looked away.

Leila pointed to a tin of tomatoes on the bench and a rusty can opener beside it. It was indeed stiff and he had to use more pressure than normal to open it.

'You should buy a new can opener,' Benny said.

'I should, but I'm an old hoarder from way back. I keep everything until it's falling to bits. Except husbands, of course.'

She cackled. Her laugh always made Benny think of the Wicked Witch of the West in The Wizard of Oz. She took his face in her hands and planted a juicy kiss on his lips.

'Thank-you darling! What would I do without you?' She placed a chopping board and a knife in front of him and handed him a clove of garlic. 'Now you can be my kitchen hand.'

When the dinner was cooked, they ate it at the kitchen table to the background music of Creedence Clearwater Revival. Benny shovelled his spaghetti into his mouth while Leila ate daintily, twirling the spaghetti around her fork. She had her usual glass of champagne and Benny had a ginger beer. The garlic bread melted on his tongue, and once he started eating it, he couldn't stop. Leila only ate one piece so Benny gobbled up the rest.

He leaned back in his chair. 'That was nice. I'm very full now.'

Sweet Hitchhiker was playing on the stereo. 'I saw Creedence in London in the 70s,' Leila said. 'They invited me backstage after the concert. Those boys sure know how to party.'

Leila had shown Benny photos of herself back then in her dancing costumes. It was hard to believe that the long-legged girl with the plump, rosy cheeks and curly blonde hair was really her. She was certainly beautiful enough to be invited back stage by a famous rock band.

Leila got up from her chair and reached out her hand to Benny. 'Come on, let's dance.'

'I'm no good at dancing,' Benny said.

'Bullshit, anyone can dance. Come on, I'll show you. '

She took his arm and led him into the living room. Benny felt awkward, as if his limbs didn't belong to him, as she arranged him into waltz position. She began moving around the room, her body close to him.

'Follow me,' she said. Wasn't the woman supposed to follow the man? He didn't know what to do anyway, so he tried to follow her moves, now and then getting out of step and treading on her toes. Leila just smiled and moved her body closer, grinding her hips into his in time with the music. Benny tried hard to think of something, anything, to stop himself from becoming aroused. But as usual, his body didn't take any notice of his mind.

Leila unlocked her hand from his, unbuttoned his shirt and ran her hands over his stomach. Benny felt self-conscious about the extra blubber on his belly, but her touch was exciting.

'You're a very sexy man, Benny,' Leila breathed into his ear. She stroked his erect penis inside his shorts until he felt as if he were going to explode, then she took him by the hand and led him into the bedroom.

After some frantic tearing off of clothes, they were both naked on her bed and Leila was bouncing energetically up and down on top of him in time to Bad Moon Rising. But this time Benny wasn't thinking about Auntie Fran.

In his mind it was Olivia on top of him, her blue eyes fixed on his, her small breasts bobbing, her hair a thick, blonde curtain around her face.

And afterwards as he and Leila lay damp and sweating on the bed, Benny imagined it was Olivia lying there with her arm across his chest, sated and happy. Once Leila fell asleep and started snoring, which she usually did after drinking champagne, Benny stayed for a while, savouring the fantasy of him and Olivia curled up together.

CHAPTER 7

After dinner each night, Benny made his way to Olivia's cottage, hid in the bushes near her kitchen window and watched her until it was time to go to work. He was afraid that if he didn't keep her in his vision, she would fade away, like a dream you tried to remember the next day.

He watched her pottering around the kitchen, cooking dinner and eating it as she scrolled through her phone. When she went into the living room, he crept around to the other side of the cottage and peered through the slit in the shutters, though this was risky, as she only had to look up in his direction to spot him. And that would ruin everything. She'd think he was a creep and never want to see him again.

Usually she watched TV while painting her fingernails or toenails or talking on her phone. Some nights he waited until 8 o'clock before she arrived home in her gym gear, and then he only had an hour of watching her before it was time to go home and get ready for work.

But he didn't care about the discomfort of crouching in the bushes; the branches scraping his face, the leaves tickling him and the cramp in his leg. He got a thick, furry feeling in the back of his throat as he watched her; everything she did was so graceful and so perfect.

On the Friday night before he was due to mow her lawn again, he almost didn't go. He had a headache and his nose was snuffly. And he would be seeing her the next day anyway. But he decided a walk might clear his head. And he had a strange, niggly feeling inside him, and a voice in his head was saying, 'You have to go.'

It was a pleasant walk; a cool breeze had taken the edge off the warm night. Darkness was just closing in as he turned into Olivia's street. A car was coming down the road from the opposite direction and stopped outside her house. He slowed down; was it Olivia arriving home? He didn't know what sort of car she had, but not having a garage—a lot of cottages didn't—she would have to park on the street.

The driver's door opened and a man got out. Tall and slim, in jeans and T-shirt. It was Lucas. He strode in the front gate to the door and rang the bell. Benny climbed over the front fence and ran to the side of the house. He heard raised voices, then the door shutting. Benny settled into his usual spot in the shrub and peered through the kitchen window.

Olivia, in a tailored skirt and blouse, was unloading a bag of groceries. Lucas was leaning against the fridge, watching her, his arms folded.

'I thought I might book us a weekend at one of those luxury resorts on the Central Coast,' he said. 'You know, champagne and spa baths and walks along the beach, lots of time to be together and remember what it was like when we first met.'

'It will never be like when we first met,' Olivia said, thumping a bag of apples down on to the kitchen bench. 'We've both changed.'

'You've changed, I'm still the same. We agreed we wanted to have a family, we talked about it, and now you've reneged on it.'

'I haven't reneged on it, I wanted to travel first, I told you that.' She approached the refrigerator holding a bottle of orange juice. Lucas moved so she had just enough room to open the door and put the juice inside. She shook her head. 'I'm fed up with talking about this; we've had this discussion so many times before. I've had a big day and I'm tired and I want you to go.'

Lucas reached out and Olivia flinched. He brushed a wisp of hair off her face. 'I can see you're tired.' His voice was soft, but it somehow didn't match his words, as if he were faking it. 'I'll go home. Just promise me you'll think about the weekend away.'

'There's no point, Lucas, can't you just accept the marriage is over?' Her voice shook with desperation. And something else. Was it fear?

'No, I can't, Livvie. Because I love you and I'm going to fight for our marriage. I don't give up that easily.'

He put his hands on her shoulders, digging his fingers into them and staring into her eyes.

'Let go, you're hurting me!'

'Not as much as you're hurting me,' he said.

'Just leave. Otherwise I'm calling the police.'

He slapped her cheek. 'Don't you dare bring the police into this, you bitch!'

A single tear rolled down her cheek. 'Please go.' Her voice was barely above a whisper. She glanced at her phone on the kitchen table and made a move towards it. Lucas let go of her shoulders, scooped up the phone, and threw it hard on to the tiled floor. It smashed into pieces.

'You bastard,' Olivia said through gritted teeth.

'If I'm a bastard you've turned me into one,' Lucas said. He pushed her and sent her sprawling on to the floor.

Benny's chest was burning with anger. He had to do something. He crept around the house to the front door and rang the doorbell.

Silence. Had Lucas knocked her out? Or worse? The front door swung open and Lucas stood there. Looking at Benny as if he were a slimy insect that had crawled out of a log.

'Er...is Olivia in?' he stammered.

'Who the fuck are you?'

'I do her mowing for her. I just want to speak to her for a minute.'

'This is a strange time to be calling, mate. You can't speak to her, she's busy.'

Olivia appeared behind Lucas. 'Hi, Benny.' Her face was tear-stained, her hair was a mess and her cheek was red and swollen.

Lucas swung around. 'Oh, Benny!' he mimicked. 'Is this one of the boyfriends you've been hiding from me?'

'Benny mows my lawn. Not that it's any business of yours.'

'I was just passing by,' Benny said, 'and I called in to...' he wavered. He hadn't thought of what he was going to say. 'To see if you still wanted me to come tomorrow morning.'

Olivia gave a small smile. Her lips quivered. Benny's heart squeezed; how he longed to make it all better for her, to see her whole face light up with a smile. 'Yes, that will be fine.'

'Okay.' Benny cleared his throat. 'Well, I'd better be going.'

'Yes, you'd better,' Lucas said. He slammed the door in Benny's face.

Benny shuffled out through the front gate and down the street. He sensed that Lucas was watching him from the window. He'd tried to stop Lucas from hurting Olivia further, but maybe he'd made things worse if Lucas thought he was her boyfriend. He couldn't help feeling flattered that Lucas—or anybody—would think that. Of course Lucas was jealous; he was obsessed with Olivia, couldn't accept that his marriage was over and let her live her life. What a creep. A dangerous creep. If someone didn't do something, Lucas might kill Olivia.

CHAPTER 8

Benny rang the doorbell at 8.00 a.m. and waited. His headache from last night was gone, but he was still snuffly. He'd gone to work even though he didn't feel like it, because he was casual and if he didn't work, he didn't get paid. But it didn't matter; seeing Olivia was better than any medicine. He took his handkerchief out of his pocket and blew his nose.

He rang the bell again. The door opened and Olivia stood there in a bathrobe. Her cheek was still swollen and there was a bruise under her eye. She looked fragile, as if a strong wind would blow her away.

'Sorry, Benny, I slept in.' She waved her hand in the direction of the back yard. 'You know what to do. And the garden, if anything needs doing.'

Benny did the lawn, though it was hard to make the edges neat. What he needed was one of those electric edge trimmers he'd seen on the Shopping Show. Would Leila buy one if he suggested it? Probably not; she was always complaining that the pension was never enough for her. 'I'm a champagne girl living on a beer budget,' she always said, though he'd never seen her with a beer.

He pulled out a few plants from the garden that he hoped were weeds, threw them in the rubbish bin, then tapped on the back door.

Olivia opened it. She was dressed in denim shorts and a lacy blouse, and her hair was up. She'd put make-up on, but it didn't hide the bruise. Benny dropped his gaze; he didn't want to make her feel bad by staring at it.

'I've finished,' he said.

'Fantastic.' She glanced in the direction of the back yard; it seemed as if her thoughts were elsewhere. 'Would you like a cold drink? Or a cup of coffee?'

Was she just asking him to be polite and hoping he'd say no? Surely she wouldn't have offered coffee if she'd wanted him to go. 'A cup of coffee would be very nice, thank-you.'

It would take him longer to drink a cup of coffee than a cold drink, so it would give him an excuse to hang around for longer.

'Have a seat, and I'll bring it out. How do you have it?'

'Milk and two sugars please.' As he said it he looked down at the roll of belly over his shorts. Olivia was so neat and dainty, being with her made him feel big and awkward. Sugar was bad for you; he should cut it out. Right now. 'Um, hold the sugar. Just milk.'

She returned in a few minutes with two steaming mugs. 'It's just instant, I haven't fired up the coffee machine yet.'

Benny sipped his coffee. It was bitter without sugar; he couldn't help making a face. 'Is the coffee too strong for you?' Olivia asked.

'No. I've given up sugar so I'm still getting used to the taste.'

'Good for you. I wish I could do that. How long have you been off sugar?'

'About five minutes.' He hadn't meant to be funny, but Olivia laughed. It was a musical laugh, like the tinkle of piano notes, and it softened her face.

She looked serious again. 'I'm sorry Lucas was rude to you last night.'

'That's all right. I'm used to it.'

Olivia looked puzzled. 'What do you mean?'

'I'm used to people being rude to me.'

'Oh…I'm sorry to hear that.'

Benny shrugged. 'He was rude to you as well.'

Olivia let out a deep sigh. 'Yes. He has a lot on his mind at the moment. But I'm not making excuses for him, we're separated. And that's one of the reasons, the main reason really. He can't control his anger.'

'I hope he didn't give you trouble because he thought I was your boyfriend.'

He studied her. Was she disgusted that anyone would think Benny was her boyfriend? She showed no sign of it, just shook her head. 'He's very jealous, he thinks every man I talk to is a potential boyfriend. So you don't need to feel bad about that.'

'Anyway,' she said, 'I'm sure there are better things to do on a Saturday morning than talk about my problems.'

There aren't, Benny wanted to tell her. He could talk about her problems all day.

'For a start, I have to buy myself a new phone,' Olivia said. She checked her watch and stood up. So she did want him to go. Benny gulped down the rest of his coffee, but it went down the wrong way, causing a fit of coughing and spluttering.

Olivia rubbed him on the back until his coughing died down. 'I'm so sorry, Benny, I didn't mean to rush you. Are you all right?'

Benny nodded, too embarrassed to speak. There was coffee down the front of his shirt. What must she think of him—that he was a clumsy slob? Auntie Vi's voice echoed in his head. 'You're a klutz, Benny Goodchild. Next to you, a hippopotamus would look like a ballet dancer.'

As he walked back home pushing the mower, his back tingled where Olivia had rubbed it. It was the first time she'd touched him. He replayed the scene over and over in his mind, forgetting to look as he crossed the road. A van narrowly avoided him, the driver giving him an angry blast of his horn. Benny smiled and waved.

#

Over the next few nights, Lucas didn't make an appearance at Olivia's house; at least not while Benny was there. Perhaps he'd got the message at last to leave Olivia alone. But he'd said he wasn't going to give up, and Benny had a feeling in the pit of his stomach that Olivia hadn't seen the last of Lucas.

Auntie Fran had told him about the importance of gut feelings. 'Your gut knows everything. It's the repository of all knowledge.' He had to look up repository in the dictionary, which was hard when he didn't know how to spell it in the first place. 'If you want to solve a problem or make a decision, just ask your gut—it's never wrong.'

Benny had thought a lot about gut feelings. How did you know if a gut feeling was real or if it was just something you wanted so much you convinced yourself it was true? He'd tested it a few times.

'I have a gut feeling that the door of this house will be unlocked,' he'd say to himself as he was about to do a new break-in. More often than not, he was wrong. Or 'I have a gut feeling that Travis and Mick will be nice to me tonight.' That never came true. So it seemed that he couldn't force a gut feeling or pretend—his gut was too clever for that—cleverer than he was.

And his gut was right on the night he knocked on the door and interrupted Lucas' attack on Olivia. Despite his not feeling well, the voice in his head had told him to go. And now that feeling was there again; the certainty that Lucas would be back.

On the Friday morning before he was due to mow her lawn again, he was watching an episode of Law and Order on TV in Olivia's living room, lounging on the recliner with the footstool up when he heard a sound. Was that the front gate? He pressed the off button on the remote control. Keys jingled at the front door. He slammed the footstool down, leapt off the recliner and looked around wildly. He dived into the hall cupboard and closed the door just as the front door opened.

Footsteps entered, the clip clop of high heels. What was Olivia doing home at this hour? Benny was crammed in between the vacuum cleaner and the mop—he couldn't move even if he wanted to. He swallowed down the panic rising in his chest. He'd left a used tea bag in a cup on the bench—he'd had a cup of peppermint tea, which he quite liked now even though he'd hated it when he first tried it. And he'd helped himself to a couple of no-sugar peppermints and left the open bag on the bench, intending to tidy it all up before he left. A dead giveaway that someone had been in the house.

The footsteps stopped. 'Shit!' she said. She must have seen the evidence. The footsteps continued towards the back door, then after a couple of minutes, came back in his direction. He held his breath as the footsteps passed him and went in the direction of the bedroom.

What was she doing? He crossed his fingers, willing her with all his might not to decide to do some vacuuming. Would she call the police to report a break-in? They'd search the place, find him and then it would be all over.

There was no good explanation for hiding in her cupboard—Olivia would think he'd broken in to steal something, or worse. To hurt her. Either way, she would want nothing more to do with him.

Then he heard her talking. Her voice was muffled at first, then gradually become more distinct. He realised she was on the phone and moving about as she spoke. Then she stopped and he could hear her clearly. Her voice was raised in anger.

'Nothing's been stolen so it wasn't a random break-in. I know it's Lucas, it's just the sort of stupid thing he'd do to scare me. He even had a cup of peppermint tea and he doesn't even like it. I don't know how he got in, but he's pretty handy with tools so maybe he picked the lock. I'll have to ask the landlord to put stronger locks on the doors.'

There was silence, then she said, 'Yeah, I'm okay. I've checked the house, there's no-one here. I came home because I have a bad headache and I'm very tired, so I'm going to take some Panadol and have a rest.'

More silence, then, 'I can't call the police because there's no evidence it's him. And if I confront him with it he'll just deny it. Honestly, Ness, I'm fine. And yes, let's go out for a drink soon, I'll look forward to it. Bye.'

Benny listened for the sound of further footsteps. There was no more clip clopping—she must have taken off her shoes, but he could hear her bare feet padding first into the kitchen, then past him in the direction of the bedroom.

Then silence. Had she gone for a rest, as she said she would? Being tired, she might go to sleep. He crossed his fingers again. Please God, let her go to sleep. Because otherwise he was stuck in the cupboard, hot and cramped, until she went out again. Which could be hours.

He waited a few more minutes to give her time to fall asleep, then gently opened the cupboard door and edged himself out. He closed the door, then crept through the living room and the kitchen. A floorboard creaked. He stopped, his heart thumping so hard it hurt. No sound from the bedroom.

He continued on toward the back door and with painstaking slowness he turned the handle, opened it and stepped outside. He closed the door gently, strode along the side of the house and legged it over the front fence. He didn't allow himself to breathe a sigh of relief until he was around the corner.

CHAPTER 9

It was only a few hours later that Benny was once more in his usual position outside Olivia's window. He'd arrived later than usual and it was already dark. He peered into the kitchen. She wasn't there, but he could hear the TV booming out from the living room.

On the kitchen bench were two half-full, take-away containers; one was rice and the other some sort of vegetable dish. After waiting for what seemed like forever and becoming hot and uncomfortable, he still hadn't seen her. Was she so engrossed in the TV show, or had she fallen asleep? At 9.00 p.m. he reluctantly disentangled himself from the bushes and crept around the side of the house to go home.

He heard a car door slam and stopped in his tracks. A car was parked across the road and a figure that he recognised got out and walked across the road. He was carrying what looked like a can and his stride was faltering as if he were drunk. Benny crept back and flattened himself against the wall. Lucas rang the doorbell then started hammering on the door.

Benny heard the front door opening and Olivia saying, 'Go away, Lucas or I'll call the police.'

'I've got a can of paint and I'll throw it on your car if you don't let me in,' Lucas said. 'I just want to talk, Livvie.'

'I don't want to talk, just go.'

'All right, you asked for it.'

Benny poked his head around the corner and saw Lucas walking out the gate swinging the can in his hand. Then Olivia's voice, angry but shaking.

'Okay, you've got five minutes.'

Benny scuttled back to his position in the bushes. He couldn't leave now; he had to make sure Lucas wasn't going to hurt Olivia. Though how he could do that, he had no idea.

They were in the living room. He couldn't see them, but their voices were raised and he could hear them clearly. 'Make it quick,' Olivia said. 'And you're drunk.'

'I get so lonely, Livvie.' His voice had taken on a whining tone. 'I'll do whatever you want; I'll go to counselling, we can go overseas, I know you want to do that, we can take off and go travelling; we'll use our savings for that instead of a house. Please!'

He sounded as if he were about to burst into tears.

'Lucas, we've done this so many times before, and it's all right for a while, but then you let your anger get the better of you...'

'It's not my anger that's the problem. It's the things you do and say that provoke me.'

'Just stop right there,' Olivia snapped. 'I'm the one who should be angry. Why did you break into my house today? Was that supposed to scare me?'

'What are you talking about?'

'You know what I'm talking about. Breaking into my house and drinking a cup of tea and eating my peppermints and sitting on my couch. You were probably watching TV as well. A gross invasion of my privacy, not to mention a criminal offence.'

'That's ridiculous, I've been at work all day.'

'Of course I wouldn't expect you to admit to it. Anyway, your 5 minutes are up, so I'm asking you to leave.'

'I'm not going anywhere when you've accused me of something I know nothing about. Whoever was in your house today it wasn't me. So you can just apologise.'

Silence. Then Olivia gasped, 'Stop it, you're hurting me!'

Benny peered in through the kitchen window again. They were still out of view.

'Say you're sorry!' Lucas demanded.

'I'm not sorry.'

Suddenly Olivia came into Benny's vision, sprawling on the floor in the doorway from the kitchen to the living room. As she went to get up, Lucas loomed in front of her and gave her an uppercut to the jaw. Benny flinched and gritted his teeth. Olivia lay unmoving on the floor. Lucas cupped his hand to his ear. 'What? I didn't hear you.'

From below him came a feeble, gasping, 'I'm sorry!'

'I'll come back when you're in a better mood,' Lucas said. He turned on his heel and staggered out, slamming the front door.

The knot in Benny's stomach was agonising. Not only had Lucas attacked Olivia again, but it was his fault. Olivia had accused Lucas of something that he had done. It was too late now to confess, even if he could. He was responsible for causing the woman he loved to be beaten up.

The woman he loved. It had a nice ring to it—it made him feel grown up. It was different from when he was with Shona—he didn't think of her as a woman, and he didn't love her. Especially when he realised she was taking advantage of him. Loving a woman was an adult, responsible thing. You promised yourself you'd look after her and protect her. And he'd failed.

\#

On the way to work, Benny went a couple of streets out of his way to a telephone box outside a corner store. It stood huddled in the faint light of a nearby street lamp. He pushed his bike into the telephone box with him and dialled triple 0.

'Do you want police, fire or ambulance?' the operator asked.

'Police, please.'

He didn't want to call them on his mobile phone in case they could trace the call to him. Maybe that was just on TV, but he wasn't taking any chances.

A sharp voice said in his ear,' What address please?'

Address? He didn't take much notice of street names and numbers, he found his way by landmarks.

'I don't know. But she lives in Marrickville. In a blue and yellow cottage. And there's a bus stop in the street and a park across the road.'

'Are you there now?'

'No.'

'What's her name and what's the emergency?'

'Olivia Bartlett. Her husband, I mean, ex-husband was beating her up. His name is Lucas, that's all I know and he's gone now. But she's hurt.'

'Can you go back to the address?'

'No, I'm sorry I have to go.'

He hung up with a heavy feeling in his stomach. All he could hope was that the police would somehow be able to find her. There wasn't much they could do now that Lucas was gone, but maybe they could stop him from doing it again. The only way to do that would be to lock him up. Or kill him.

Benny arrived at work with a minute to spare, after racing there on his bike as if he was in the Tour de France. He punched the time clock and paused for a couple of minutes to catch his breath.

Ned came lumbering out of his office. 'Come on, bad boy! Don't just stand there! There's a truck to be unloaded in B shed!'

Benny hurried over to B shed, where a group of men, including Travis and Mick, stood around a large truck, smoking and laughing raucously. It sounded like a dirty joke type of laugh. He didn't know why Travis and Mick never got into trouble for smoking and hanging out with the drivers—he was sure that if he did it, Ned would come down on him like a ton of bricks. It was one of the many unfairnesses of life that he didn't think about because it only made him unhappy.

'Hey, bad boy!' Travis called. 'Wanna hear a joke?'

Saying no wasn't an option, Travis was going to tell him anyway.

'What's the speed limit of sex?'

Benny shrugged.

'Sixty-eight. Sixty-nine you have to turn around.'

Raucous laughter again. Benny looked at them, blank-faced.

'I don't think he understands it,' Travis hissed in a loud whisper.

'Hey bad boy, have you ever had a sixty-niner?' Mick yelled.

Benny ignored him, walked over to the forklift and clambered in. Mick strode over and stood in front of him, pointing his scruffy bearded chin at him. 'I asked you a question, buddy.'

'I don't have to answer it.'

'Yes you do.' Mick put his hand on Benny's shoulder and gripped it hard. Months of harassment, jeers and jokes exploded like one big fireball in Benny's chest.

He gave Mick a hard punch in the gut. Mick yelled and doubled over. 'You bastard!'

He sprang for Benny but Ned appeared suddenly and hauled him back. 'That's enough, mate.'

Mick pointed at Benny. 'He started it. He punched me in the gut.'

'You're not in the schoolyard now. Go to the other shed and do the bill of lading.'

Mick skulked off. 'You'll keep, bad boy,' he said over his shoulder.

Before Benny could thank Ned, he pointed a grubby, fat finger at Benny and said, 'And you, get to work.'

At tea break, Benny sat on his own sipping on his bottle of water. He hadn't had time before he left home to make himself a sandwich. As Travis and Mick went into the tearoom with the others in a boisterous laughing group, Benny was careful to avoid Mick's gaze. He didn't know what he'd meant by 'you'll keep,' but he resolved never to find himself alone with Mick.

As they came out again after the break, Travis and a couple of others veered over to the toilets. Benny got up and ambled in that direction. Travis was talking to Colin, an older man whose belly rivalled Ned's.

'I just said to her,"No way am I getting you a drink. You're so big on chicks having equal rights, you can buy your own fucking drink."'

'Travis, can I speak to you for a minute?' Benny asked.

Colin nudged Travis. 'You're in trouble now, Trav.'

'Nah,' Travis said. 'Me and Bad Boy are good mates, aren't we?'

He put his arm around Benny's shoulders and led him outside to the bike racks.

'Make it quick,' he said. 'Ned's narky tonight. I don't think he's been getting any at home.'

'I need a gun,' Benny said.

Travis narrowed his eyes. 'Why should I care?'

'I'll be your lookout in that business you were telling me about if you get me a gun. Whatever you give me for my first payment, I'll use that to pay you for it.'

'It's not that easy to get a gun,' Travis said. 'It's illegal, you know.' He sniggered.

'I know,' Benny said. 'That's my offer, take or leave it.'

He crossed his fingers behind his back, his heart hammering. He was hoping desperately that he could bluff Travis by pretending it was no big deal. If Travis suspected how much he wanted the gun, he'd make him jump through all sorts of hoops.

'You know I could just beat you to a pulp, then you'd have to do what I say, gun or no gun.'

'If you beat me to a pulp, I won't be able to be your lookout,' Benny said.

Travis grinned. 'You got a point there. What do you want the gun for?'

'I can't tell you. Don't ask me any questions about the gun, and I won't ask you any about your business.'

Travis put out his hand. 'You're smarter than you look, bad boy. You've got a deal. '

CHAPTER 10

Benny wasn't sure when the idea first came to him. It had probably been lurking in the back of his mind for some time. But as he cycled to work that night after calling the police, the idea was there, as clear as a drop of water shining in the sun. And his gut was in agreement; chiming like church bells, drowning out all doubts and fears. The only way to guarantee Olivia's safety was to kill Lucas.

On the forklift, he'd mulled over the various methods of killing him – strangling him, clubbing him to death or poisoning him. But they all sounded too difficult or complicated. There were too many things that could go wrong.

He'd seen a movie once where a man wanted to kill his brother so he could inherit the family fortune. So he went to his brother's house late at night and when the brother came to the front door, he made him go into the living room at gunpoint and shot him. He then emptied cupboards and drawers on to the floor to make it look as if his brother had surprised a burglar. To cement the burglary story, he forced the back door open and took his brother's wallet and a few other valuables. After leaving he threw the gun and the things he'd stolen into a river.

It sounded like a foolproof plan. Admittedly Benny had never used a gun, but how hard could it be? Just aim it and pull the trigger. That's how Clint and Errol and John did it. Benny just had to trust that Travis would find him one. In the crime shows on TV the drug trade criminals always had guns—surely Travis would know someone who could sell Benny a gun, no questions asked.

Benny mulled over his plan as he showered and changed and downed a bowl of cereal. The hardest part would be arriving and leaving without anyone seeing him. In the movie, the brother had eventually got caught because someone had noticed his car parked around the corner, and had seen him get out and walk towards the house. Benny wouldn't make that mistake—he didn't have a car, and being on foot was always better. Easier to escape and hide if you had to. He had become an expert at bolting and hiding when he was in his teens, and a neighbour or some other busybody spotted him doing a break-in. Though he was slimmer and fitter back then.

As soon as he finished his breakfast, he went out into the garden shed to get the mower.

'Hey, Benny!'

Leila was leaning over the back balcony, a mug in her hand, wearing a dress that looked like a lot of rags all sewn together. Boho chic, she called it.

'You've been neglecting me lately.'

Benny's heart sank. Surely she didn't want sex now—straight after breakfast? He couldn't anyway, he was due at Olivia's in a few minutes.

'The lawn!' She swept her arm out over the yard. 'It's a jungle! I'm too scared to set foot in it; I might be attacked by a wild animal!'

'I'm sorry, I'll do it this afternoon.'

'Where are you going with that?'

'To mow a lawn. For a friend.'

'Would that friend happen to be female?'

'Yes.' Benny felt his cheeks warm. Why couldn't he lie and say no?

'Oh really? I'm jealous.'

What could he say to that? There was no comparison between Leila and Olivia. They might as well be from different planets; it was even hard to believe they were of the same sex.

Leila threw back her head and let out a raucous laugh. 'Look at your face, it's priceless! I was joking, honey. I think it's wonderful that you have a girlfriend. About time, I say.'

'Oh.' Benny was tongue-tied. 'Thank-you.'

'Well you'd better get going. Don't want to keep her waiting!'

#

When Benny knocked on the front door, Olivia opened the door just a crack and hiding behind it, said, 'Hi Benny, go ahead and start.'

He finished the lawn, breaking his own record, and pulled out a few weeds from the garden. Sweat was pouring off him—in his haste to get there on time he'd forgotten his water bottle. He knocked on the back door, calling out, 'I've finished!'

The door opened and Olivia stood there in a flowery summer dress. Benny's heart clenched as he took in her swollen, bruised jaw and red, puffy cheek. Despite her injuries, she looked like an angel—an angel who needed a knight in shining armour to ride in on his horse, kill the baddie and spirit her away to live happily ever after.

He didn't have any armour, or a horse, but a little part of him dared to hope that the rest of the fairy tale might come true.

'Oh, look at you!' Olivia said. 'Let me get you a drink!'

She went inside and returned with a small bottle of ginger beer. How did she know it was his favourite soft drink? He overcame the temptation to down it all in one gulp.

She sat opposite him. 'You didn't happen to be walking past my house last night, did you?'

Benny broke out in another sweat, willing himself to look surprised rather than guilty. 'No, I was at home watching TV.'

She nodded, as if that was the answer she expected. When it seemed as if she wasn't going to say anything more, Benny said, 'Why?'

He had a fair idea why, but figured it was a reasonable question for an innocent person to ask.

Her lips quivered; she looked on the verge of tears. 'I may as well tell you; I guess it's pretty obvious. Lucas was here last night and he attacked me. The police came around after he left; someone had reported it. They wouldn't tell me who, but I got the impression they didn't know. I guess it was one of the neighbours, though I didn't think we were loud enough for them to hear.'

'It's good they did,' Benny said. 'He shouldn't treat you like that.'

'You think?' Her tone was hard, tinged with bitterness. 'He wasn't like that when we married, you know. He was the sweetest, most charming man you could meet. He always had a quick temper but he never laid a hand on me until he got the promotion to project manager. There was a lot of stress and frustration in the job and he took it all out on me.'

'I know what you mean,' Benny said. 'My Auntie Vi used to beat me till I was bleeding for not making my bed properly. Then later on Auntie Fran told me it was because she was really unhappy. She was in love with her best friend, but her best friend never knew and she went away and Auntie Vi never saw her again. I don't know why people have to hurt other people when they're unhappy.'

'I don't know either.' She looked at him.' Where were your parents?'

'I didn't have a father. My mum died when I was three. She killed herself.'

Olivia gasped and put her hand to her mouth. 'How terrible for you!'

'I don't remember her, but Auntie Fran said she was sick.' He pointed to his head. 'In the head.'

'So your Auntie Fran brought you up?'

'And Auntie Rose and Auntie Vi. They all took it in turns to look after me, but I liked Auntie Fran the best.'

Benny finished his drink and put the bottle on the table. He didn't want to go, had to keep her talking.

'Where are your mum and dad?' he blurted out.

'In Perth. I was brought up there.'

'Do you miss them?'

'Yes, I do, especially my mum. She annoys me when she nags me, but I know it's because she worries about me. She's never liked Lucas, she said there was something about him that she didn't trust, and she was relieved when we broke up.'

'Are the police going to arrest him?' Benny asked. If the police arrested Lucas and put him in jail for a long time, Benny wouldn't have to kill him.

'They said they're going to talk to him. And they advised me to take an AVO out against him; they said if I didn't, they would.'

'What's an AVO?'

'Apprehended Violence Order. It's a legal document saying what Lucas can and can't do. Like he can't contact me or come to my house without my permission. I've been on the verge of doing it many times. But the police don't know him like I do. It won't stop him.'

'He seems a bit crazy to me,' Benny said.

Olivia looked at him with surprise. 'What makes you say that? You've only met him for a couple of minutes.'

Whoops. He wasn't about to tell Olivia he'd been hiding outside her window for days on end. 'Just a feeling I have,' he stammered.

'You're right though, I think he is a bit off his rocker. You're pretty perceptive, aren't you?'

Benny's cheeks warmed. He didn't know what perceptive meant, but it sounded like a compliment.

'I'll tell you a secret,' Olivia said, 'if you promise not to tell anyone.'

'Cross my heart and hope to die.' Benny made a solemn cross on his heart. He loved it when people told him secrets, it made him feel special. It didn't happen very often, though. People thought that because he wasn't smart, he couldn't be trusted not to blurt them out.

'I'm going to London in a few weeks. I've been saving my money and I'm going to pack up and move there. Lucas will never find me.'

Benny's heart plummeted to his feet. Just when he'd found her, she was going away!

'Are you going forever?'

She smiled. 'Forever's a long time. But certainly for a couple of years at least. Long enough for Lucas to realise it's over and move on.'

A couple of years! It may as well be forever. This was the worst secret ever.

'Benny, don't look so sad!'

'I'll miss (he stopped himself in time from saying 'you') mowing your lawn.'

'I'll miss you doing it too. I probably won't even have a lawn in London.'

As Benny trundled back home with the mower, he was oblivious to the sun beating down on his head and the woman with her two children walking towards him whom he literally almost mowed down. There was only one thought in his head—he now had one more reason to kill Lucas. If Lucas was dead, Olivia would have no need to go to London.

CHAPTER 11

Clint Eastwood was riding towards the bad man's home. He was going to free Marisol, the damsel in distress, who was being held prisoner by the bad guys. Benny knew what was going to happen; he'd seen the movie A Fistful of Dollars countless times.

Clint Eastwood was going to shoot the guards, mess up the house to make it look as it was the Sheriff who did it, and then give Marisol some money to escape. The only part about the story that Benny didn't like was that Clint, The Man With No Name, didn't end up with the girl—she was already married and had a son.

Maybe that made Clint a better person than he—he was saving Marisol's life because he was a hero and not because he wanted to be with her.

Clint made it look so easy, handling the gun as if he were born with it. At work the night before, as they were going for their tea break, Travis muttered in Benny's ear, 'The eagle is landing next Wednesday night.'

Benny looked at him, puzzled.

'The job, you fuckwit,' Travis hissed.

'Oh.' Benny nodded. 'When will I get…' he glanced around him, 'that thing I asked you for?'

'Patience, bad boy. You've got to do the job first.'

It was hard to be patient. Now that he'd made the decision, Benny wanted to do it now. How much time did he have? Olivia had said she was going to London in a few weeks. How long was a few?

Benny put the DVD on pause and went into the kitchen to fix himself some breakfast. He pulled the packet of Cocopops out of the cupboard, then stopped. He was supposed to be giving up sugar. If he wanted Olivia to fall in love with him he should smarten up, lose some weight, start working out. He was pretty sure that Clint Eastwood wouldn't eat Cocopops. Benny shoved the Cocopops back in the cupboard and put a saucepan of water on the stove to boil some eggs.

There was a knock on his back door. 'Benny, can you come up for a minute?'

Benny felt a niggle of irritation. He went to the door and called out,' I'm sick, I've got a cold.'

'It will only take a minute, I promise.'

He wished he could pluck up the courage to say no. Not no to helping her, but no to what came after. But he couldn't—he knew what it was like to be lonely.

He opened the door. Leila stood there in her gown and slippers. 'I just need you to get something out of the top cupboard for me. My vertigo's bad today.'

She'd never mentioned vertigo before. He followed her up the stairs and into the house. Remembering he was supposed to have a cold, Benny coughed and sniffled a couple of times. Leila pointed to the step ladder in front of the hall cupboard. 'Could you get me the new pillows from the top shelf? My night sweats have ruined the ones I'm using.'

Benny climbed up the step ladder, hauled out the pillows, still in their plastic wrappings and handed them to her.

'Thank-you, you're a sweetheart.' She put them in the bedroom, then came back and said, 'I'm cooking Persian eggs for breakfast. Would you like to stay and have some?'

It sounded a lot more appetising than boiled eggs, but of course he knew where the Persian eggs would lead to.

He gave another sniff. 'No, thank-you. I'd better go back downstairs and get some sleep. For my cold,' he added.

Leila stood in front of him and stroked his face. 'You poor thing. I know just the thing to help you sleep.'

Her other hand moved down and started stroking his crotch. Benny pulled away. There was only one way to deal with this—tell the truth. That's what Auntie Fran said. 'Always tell the truth. Sometimes it hurts, but it hurts even more if the person finds the truth out later themselves.'

'I'm sorry, Leila,' he stammered, 'but I can't. I have a girlfriend now.'

Okay, it wasn't true right now, but it was going to be. And surely telling the truth before you needed to was a good thing. Even better than waiting till it happened.

'I know that, honey. You told me. I think it's fabulous. But that's got nothing to do with you and me.'

Benny looked at her, shocked. 'Yes it does. It's wrong to do that stuff with someone else if you have a girlfriend.'

Somehow he couldn't bring himself to say the word sex, and he would never say 'fuck' or 'screw' like the guys at work did.

She gave him a soft kiss on the cheek. 'You're so adorably innocent. And I find that an incredible turn-on.'

She opened her gown. She was naked underneath. And she'd shaved her female bits, so there was only a thin line of hair up the middle.

Benny looked away. 'I can't, Leila.'

'You know, I could rent out your room in a heartbeat, darling, but I don't want to. I like you, Benny, I like you a lot and you're a good tenant.'

It took a few moments for her words to sink in. 'Do you mean you'll throw me out if I don't go to bed with you?'

Leila reached out and began to undo the top button of his jeans. 'I'm sure it won't come to that. You've got a good deal here and I know you wouldn't want to throw it all away.'

Benny pushed her hand away and did up his button over the bulge in his jeans. 'I already said I can't. And if you throw me out, that's all right. I'll find somewhere else.'

It was true and it felt good to say it. Once Travis paid him the money for the job, he could easily find somewhere else to live. Somewhere much better than this—with a swimming pool and a gym so he could get fit. And without a sex-crazed landlady living above him.

Leila's lips tightened and her eyes were as hard as pebbles. 'No you won't, you silly boy. You won't find anywhere as cheap as this and as soon as they see that you're retarded, you won't stand a chance.'

The shock of it was like a bucket of cold water in the face. It was the first time Leila had ever said that word. Retarded. The word that had haunted him all his life—throughout school, all the jobs he'd had, from random people in the street.

'You'll get used to it,' Auntie Fran had said to him once when he came home from school in tears. 'You can't stop people from saying it, so you have to control how you react to it. You have to get tough on the inside. Like a tortoise has a tough shell on the outside to protect him, you have to grow a shell on the inside.'

But no matter how hard he tried, he couldn't grow a shell on the inside. Every time someone called him a retard, or a dumbass or any of the other words that meant the same thing, it was as if they'd shot an arrow into his chest.

And the worst part was that he'd thought Leila was his friend. Without a word he turned, opened the door and stumbled down the stairs. When he went into the kitchen, he discovered the bottom of the saucepan was burnt and the water had boiled dry.

#

Benny had a strange feeling in his stomach as he rode to work on Wednesday night. The same feeling he'd had before exam time at school, as if he needed to go to the toilet. He'd always failed his exams, but he couldn't afford to fail at this job for Travis and Mick.

He had no idea what they would be doing while he was the lookout—it was something to do with drugs, and if they got caught and arrested by the police, they would probably go to jail and Travis wouldn't be able to get him the gun.

'You're at Shed B to help unpack,' Ned told Benny after he clocked in. As he headed in that direction, he felt a hand on his shoulder. 'I'll come and get you when we're ready,' Travis muttered in his ear. 'I'll give old Ned a chance to get himself a cup of tea and his porno mag.'

'What do I have to do?'

'I'll tell you when the time comes. Chill, bad boy. It's all good.'

All good. Benny hated that expression. People usually said it when everything was about to turn bad. He went over to the stack of large cardboard boxes in the corner of the shed. They'd all been opened to have the bill of lading done, and now the contents had to be unpacked and stored to fulfil store orders.

He took out the first box and opened it. It was full of candles wrapped in cellophane. He picked up a pink one and held it to his nose. It smelt of strawberries, and instantly it took him back to the packets of strawberry lollies he'd shoplifted from the corner shop on his way home from school. Stealing was the only thing he was good at—he would have received an A+ for that.

'You're supposed to stack them on the shelves, not get high on them,' Ned said, as he walked off towards the office. His movements were predictable— he did his rounds at the beginning of the shift, then sat in his office with the TV on and his porno stash. Every so often he'd come out, check what everyone was doing, then disappear into his office again.

Benny began stacking the boxes of candles on to the metal shelves. After Ned had done his second round and disappeared into his office, Travis appeared at Benny's shoulder. 'You're on.'

He pointed to the doorway of the shed. 'Go hang around there. If you see Ned coming, cough loudly three times, that's the signal. Then distract him.'

'How?'

'I dunno, ask him to explain something to you, be your usual dumb self. You'll think of something.' Travis clapped him on the shoulder. 'We'll be as quick as two rabbits fucking.'

He disappeared to the opposite back corner of the shed. Benny went over to the front entrance of the shed, from where he could see Ned's office. He gazed up at the inky black sky sprinkled with stars. If he looked hard enough, he could see his Mum's face smiling down at him from one of the stars. Auntie Vi told him his Mum had gone to heaven to be a star, and was watching over him from above. On summer nights he lay on the lawn looking up at the stars, wondering which one she was.

'She loved you very much, Benny,' Auntie Vi said. 'But God loved her too and called her away.'

When he went to live with Auntie Rose, she snorted when Benny repeated this to her. 'Don't believe anything Vivian tells you. God didn't call your Mum away, she killed herself. And if she'd loved you, she wouldn't have done it.' But Benny put his hands over his ears and refused to listen.

Benny shifted from one foot to the other. What were Travis and Mick doing? He peered around a stack of boxes to the corner of the shed. Travis had a screw driver and was unscrewing the top off a toy drum. He took out a rectangular package, handed it to Mick who put it in a sports bag at his feet. Travis screwed the top back on and pulled another drum out of the box.

Drugs, as he'd suspected. What were they planning to do with them? In the latest TV episode of Crime Lords, the drug smuggler had visited his contact in the dead of night and was given a large suitcase of money. Would Travis give Benny his money in a suitcase?

As Travis looked up, Benny quickly ducked behind the boxes. He'd be angry if he saw Benny watching him. Benny returned to his lookout spot just in time to see Ned ambling in his direction, talking on his mobile phone. He hadn't seen Benny yet and if he kept going in the direction he was going, he only had to look inside the shed to see Travis and Mick.

Benny racked his brain. What could he do? He stepped out into Ned's path. Ned stopped abruptly. 'Bad boy, what are you doing? Get back to work.'

'Talk to you later,' he said into the phone and put it in his pocket.

'I have a headache,' Benny said. 'Do you have any Panadol?'

Ned pointed in the direction of his office. 'In the second drawer of my desk. Help yourself.'

He started off again. 'Can you come with me?' Benny blurted out in desperation. 'I'm feeling sick, like I'm going to faint.'

Ned looked at him with concern. 'You should go home if you're feeling that ill.'

Benny shook his head. 'I just need some Panadol.'

'All right, come with me. You can sit down for a while in my office.'

Ned took his arm. Benny remembered he was supposed to warn Travis and Mick and gave three loud coughs before Ned led him to the office. It was poky and smelt of body odour and greasy food. The desk was cluttered with messy piles of paper, and on the wall was a calendar with a photo of a young blonde in a skimpy bikini licking an ice-cream cone.

Benny quickly looked away, but not before he noticed the ice cream was chocolate, his favourite. Ned rummaged around in his desk drawer and pulled out a battered packet of Panadol. 'I suppose you want a glass of water, too.'

He went down the corridor to the tea room and came back with a glass of water. He handed it to Benny and watched him as he swallowed the pills. Benny took his time, wondering what do to next to detain Ned. Had Travis and Mick had enough time to finish what they were doing?

'I think I would feel better if I had a cup of tea,' Benny said.

'So I suppose you want me to make it for you and bring it on a silver platter. This is not the bloody Sheraton. Smoko's in an hour, you can wait till then.'

Panic was rising in Benny's chest. What if Travis and Mick hadn't finished? In a last ditch effort, he put his hand on his forehead and sank into Ned's chair. 'I'm feeling a bit dizzy.'

'That's it, I'm sending you home. I can't have you passing out on the job. I'll call you a taxi—or maybe an ambulance.'

'No, a taxi will be good,' Benny said hurriedly.

Ned picked up the phone and rang for a taxi. He stayed with Benny until it arrived—it only took a few minutes. There was nothing more Benny could do now; he couldn't stop Ned from sending him home, so he could only hope that Travis and Mick had heard his cough and sped things up.

As Benny got into the taxi, Ned said, 'If you're well enough you can come back in the morning and pick up your bike. If not, phone me and I'll organise someone to drop it off to you.'

Guilt prickled Benny all the way home. He'd lied to Ned about being sick, but Ned had believed him and taken care of him. The others all laughed at Ned behind his back because he was fat and lazy, and he was often gruff, but he was the only person on Benny's shift at Lotus Flower who treated him like a normal person.

CHAPTER 12

Benny walked to work the next morning, collected his bike and on the way home called into Olivia's house, letting himself in with his key as usual. He was on a mission—to find evidence of Lucas's address. All he knew of Lucas was his name and that he was a project manager.

He went straight into the study and systematically went through the papers on the desk and in the drawers. Nothing with Lucas's name on it. He rifled through the wastepaper basket.

Junk mail, tissues and an apple core. And a crumpled envelope. It was empty, addressed to Mr and Mrs L Bartlett 125 Greygum Ave Newtown. It was funny to think of Olivia as Mrs L Bartlett; it made her sound like an old, married lady. She was no longer at that address, but maybe Lucas was. Benny shoved the envelope in his pocket.

#

In the late afternoon Benny took the train from Marrickville to Newtown, after the assistant at the ticket window directed him to the right platform. It was crammed with people coming home from work and he had to strap-hang, feeling self-conscious about his sweaty armpits.

Once out of Newtown Station, he took out his iPhone from his pocket. He wasn't a big phone user, not like lots of people he saw who couldn't seem to tear themselves away from their phones. Benny wasn't into Facebook or any other social media-to him it was just a blur of confusing images, jokes he didn't understand and people saying nasty things. The one thing he did find his phone useful for, however, was giving directions. He couldn't read maps to save his life and Siri did come in handy for that.

'Hey Siri, find 125 Greygum Avenue,' he said.

'Finding 125 Greygum Avenue,' Siri droned. Then, 'Proceed along King St and take the first right turn.'

It turned out that Greygum Avenue was a few blocks from the station and Benny was hot and tired by the time he found it. Someone on the train had said it was the hottest summer Sydney had ever had and it certainly felt like it.

Number 125 was a faded terrace house fronting the footpath, wedged in between terrace houses on either side. It was 5.30 p.m., too early for lights, so there was no way of knowing if Lucas, or whoever the occupant was, was home. There was also nowhere where Benny could loiter without being seen.

He pulled his cap down over his face, strolled to the end of the street where he could still see the house, and stood under the shade of a plane tree. He took his phone out and scrolled through the screen looking at all the apps he didn't use. No one would look twice, he hoped, at someone glued to his phone, and they'd assume he was waiting for someone.

He'd been there an hour, and his leg was cramping and his stomach was rumbling, when a dark blue sedan stopped at Number 125. A tall, slender man carrying a briefcase got out and opened the front gate. Even from that distance Benny could see it was Lucas. He unlocked the front door and went inside. Benny did a jubilant fist pump. He'd found Lucas—he hadn't expected it to be so easy.

Then a thought occurred to him. The houses were so close together, his neighbours were bound to hear the gunshot when he killed Lucas. He would need a silencer. He'd seen them in movies; if Travis could get a gun, surely he could get a silencer as well.

#

When Benny went to the shed to get the lawn mower, he found a padlock on it. When had that appeared? He walked up the back steps and knocked on the door. Leila whipped it open. She was in a cotton nightie, her hair out in a woolly mop.

'Leila, why is there a padlock on the shed door?'

'Because, darling, if you want to go and cut your girlfriend's grass, you can buy your own lawn mower.'

She went inside and slammed the door. What was the matter with her? Was she still mad at him about the other night? Surely not, that was ages ago. Or it seemed ages ago, anyway. And if he couldn't get into the shed, he couldn't mow her lawn either.

Today was his Saturday for seeing Olivia and there was no way he was missing out on that. He'd just have to go without the lawn mower.

When she opened the front door, he blurted out, 'I'm sorry, I can't do your lawn today. My lawn mower has broken down and I have to get a new one.'

He felt bad telling her a lie and looked down at his feet, so she couldn't see the guilt on his face.

'Oh, that's bad luck,' Olivia said. 'Is your mower not repairable?'

Benny shook his head.

'Never mind, the lawn can wait. Would you like to come in and have a coffee?'

She was inviting him inside! Benny's heart fluttered. 'I'd like that.' He stepped inside, then remembering his manners, said, ' Thank you.'

It was as familiar as his own home, but he had to pretend he'd never been there. 'A nice place you have here,' he said.

'It's cosy, isn't it? Just right for one person.'

Benny sat at her kitchen table and watched her making the coffee in her coffee machine. He would have been just as happy with instant, but it gave him a warm feeling all over to see her going to all this trouble for him. It meant she liked him.

She brought over the mugs and sat down opposite him.

'How has your week been, Benny?' she asked.' Apart from your lawn mower breaking down?'

'Very good,' he said.

'Did you work last night?'

Benny nodded. He thought back to his arrival at the warehouse. Travis had given him the thumbs up after he punched the time clock. 'All good,' he said. 'Great work. Hope you're feeling better.' He gave him a wink.

Benny pulled him aside. 'Can you get me a silencer as well?' he whispered.

'Who do you think I am? Santa Claus? Do you even know how to use one?'

What did he mean? A silencer or a gun? The answer was no to both.

Travis grimaced. 'I thought so.'

'How long before I get the money and the you-know-what?' Benny said, looking nervously around him.

'Quit looking like that,' Travis said in a low voice. 'It makes people suspicious. Just pretend we're having a normal conversation, but keep your voice down. And to answer your question, we haven't got the money ourselves yet, so just chill.'

But it was hard to chill when he didn't know how much time he had.

'How was it?' Olivia asked.

'How was what?'

She smiled. 'Work, of course.'

'Oh.' Benny shrugged. 'Okay.'

He glanced at her, then looked down at the table. 'When are you going to London?'

'In four weeks,' she replied. 'I'm getting really excited. I've never been to Europe and living in London will be a dream come true. Just imagine, I'll be able to catch the Eurostar train to Paris for the weekend!'

It certainly did sound exciting. The only things Benny knew about Paris were the Eiffel Tower and croissants, and he'd heard of people eating snails, which made his stomach turn. And looking at the way Olivia's eyes lit up when she spoke about it, he realised with a heavy feeling that even with Lucas dead, she would still go.

As he walked home, the thought came to him. What was to stop him going too? Once Travis had paid him for the job, he'd have money to burn. The thought of going to a foreign country by himself filled him with dread and excitement at the same time. It would be worth it, though, to see her again. Somehow, before she left, he'd have to find out where she was staying.

CHAPTER 13

It had been a week since they'd done the job and still Benny had received nothing from Travis. 'Quit hassling me,' he said after Benny asked him about it again. 'I'll tell you when I've got it.'

But Benny was running out of patience. 'Come on, Travis, where is it?' Travis was doing the bill of lading, ticking off a list of items on the iPad.

'Don't interrupt, I'm busy. There's another job on next week. You'll get it then.'

Frustration burned in Benny's chest. Why was it taking so long? Not wanting to make Travis any angrier, he approached Mick, who was on forklift duty. Remembering Mick's threat after Benny had punched him in the stomach, Benny didn't get too close. 'Mick, why is it taking so long for you to get the money and the other thing?'

Mick shrugged. 'Dunno. Trav's running the show, ask him.'

He turned the forklift around and drove off with his load. 'This is Olivia's life you're messing with!' Benny wanted to yell at him.

At tea break, Benny sat on the concrete at the doorway of the shed, munching his sandwich and watching the steady stream of headlights passing by on the road. He'd gone to Olivia's house as usual before work. He had an extra reason to go there now apart from wanting to feel close to her—he was her protector. Her knight in shining armour, without the armour.

If Lucas arrived and started beating her up, he would knock on the door again to stop him, or call the police. But Lucas hadn't turned up. Maybe the AVO that Olivia said she was going to put into place was stopping him, even though she didn't think it would.

Whatever the reason, Benny was glad. Much as he liked the idea of being her protector, he liked even more watching her graceful movements as she pottered around the kitchen, preparing her dinner.

In his imagination Olivia and he were a couple. As she came through the front door after work, Benny hurried out, gave her a kiss on the lips, and poured her a glass of wine. She sat at the kitchen table while he cooked dinner, telling him about her day. He'd have to brush up on his cooking—somehow he couldn't see her sitting down to baked beans on toast.

They ate it by candlelight and afterwards they cuddled up on the couch and watched TV together. He didn't care what they watched, anything she chose was fine by him. He felt the weight of her head on his shoulder, her body soft and supple under his arm. Then they walked arm-in-arm to the bedroom.

His vision stopped abruptly, as if he were watching a movie and it cut to another scene. Making love to Olivia would be so wonderful that his mind couldn't picture it. It would be the closest he would get to heaven. If God knew what he was planning to do—and he'd been taught at school that God was everywhere and knew everything—he would have already put Benny on the Heaven Blacklist.

#

It was Benny's turn on the forklift. He began unloading the pallets off the truck and into the warehouse. Travis was unpacking boxes that had arrived earlier. Mick was nowhere to be seen. Ned poked his head around the corner.

'Where's Mick?' he asked. Travis shrugged. 'Running late maybe.'

But 30 minutes later, Mick still hadn't arrived. Ned reappeared. 'He's not answering his phone.'

'Dunno what the problem is,' Travis said. 'Maybe he went out cruising and got lucky.' He said it as if it was meant to be a joke, but his grin turned into a scowl.

'Well, you boys are on your own. The others are in Shed A. Call me if you need me.'

'I need you like I need a dose of the clap,' Travis muttered to Ned's retreating back.

'Why isn't Mick here?' Benny asked.

'Fucked if I know,' Travis said. 'I'll have to do the job myself. I'll need you to be lookout again; I'll give you the nod in about ten.'

In ten minutes he came over and gestured to Benny to come down off the forklift. 'I'll be over there,' he gestured to the corner of the warehouse where he had been unpacking the boxes. 'I've got to put the stuff in my car and it's parked on the street, so you will have to keep watch until I get back.'

Benny took up his position at the entrance of the shed. He glanced back at Travis, who deftly unscrewed the lid off a toy piano, took out a plastic bag and put it in a sports bag beside him. Travis looked up and saw him watching. He scowled and pointed to the door of the shed.

Benny looked back towards the office. There was a light in the window, but the curtains were drawn so he couldn't see Ned. He crossed his fingers that Ned would stay there. He didn't want to have to pretend he was sick again, but he couldn't think of any other way to distract him. He checked his watch. Ten minutes had passed. Hurry up, Travis! He turned his head in Travis's direction, enough to see that he and the bag had disappeared. Good, he must be putting the bag in his car.

In a couple of minutes, Travis was by his side, breathless. 'All done. I need you to do something for me.' He lowered his voice. 'Keep the stash for me for a couple of days.'

Benny stared at him. 'Stash? You mean the drugs?'

Travis clamped his hand over Benny's mouth. It was damp and smelt of cigarette smoke. 'For fuck's sake! Do you want to tell the whole world?'

'There's only us and Ned, and he's in his office,' Benny said.

'You don't know who might be snooping around. Listen, when we've finished work I'm going to drop you and your bike at your place and give you the stash.'

'Why do I have to keep it?' Benny asked.

'I think the cops might have picked up Mick, that's the only reason he wouldn't be here today. He knew the job was on tonight. I know he won't squeal but I can't have the stuff at my place in case the cops start sniffing around. It'll be safe at yours; they'll never associate you with me.'

Benny went cold all over. The cops! No way could he afford to get caught. He saw himself in jail, looking out through the bars to the other prison cells lining the corridor, while Olivia boarded the plane and jetted off to the other side of the world.

He'd heard horrible things about what went on in jails, things that made his stomach turn. If he'd thought about the police before, he'd dismissed it from his mind. He was just the lookout—surely he wouldn't go to jail for that. But now Travis was trying to drag him into it, make him as guilty as he and Mick.

'How do you know they won't?' he said. 'We work at the same place.'

'Because they'll deduce you don't have enough brains to be involved in a business like this.'

'I don't want it at my place. Can't you find somewhere else to hide it?'

'I'm the one calling the shots,' Travis snarled. 'Do you want your money and weapon or not?'

Benny stared at him, shoulders slumped.

'Good man, it's just for a couple of days. Until I can find out what's going on with Mick.'

CHAPTER 14

Travis pulled up in front of Benny's flat at 7.15 a.m. 'Big place you've got.'

'It's not mine,' Benny said. 'I just live in the downstairs flat.'

They got out and Travis opened the boot of his station wagon and hauled out Benny's bike. He pulled out the spare tyre and a spanner and undid the nuts, revealing a hidden storage place underneath. He pulled out the sports bag, replaced the storage cover and the tyre and slammed the boot shut.

An upstairs window opened and Leila's head appeared. She waved to Benny, then stopped when she saw Travis.

'Who's your friend, Benny?' she called out.

'Jason!' Travis called out. 'Nice to meet you!'

Benny waved back to Leila and followed Travis through his front gate, wheeling his bike. He unlocked the front door, wheeled his bike into the living room and propped it up against the wall.

'Was that your old lady?' Travis asked.

'No, my landlady.'

'Hope she's not going to poke her nose in where it don't belong,' Travis said.

'She doesn't come in here,' Benny said. He didn't know that for sure— she could if she wanted to, she had a key. But why would she want to?

Benny took the bag from Travis and went into his bedroom. He took the lid off his laundry basket and shoved the bag inside on top of his dirty clothes. If Leila decided to come snooping, this would hopefully be the last place she would look.

When he came back out, Travis was looking at the photo of his mother on the mantelpiece. 'Is this your girlfriend?'

'No, it's my mother.'

Travis's eyebrows shot up. 'You're kidding me!' He whistled. 'What a MILF!'

Benny looked puzzled. 'MILF?'

'Mother I'd love to fuck. Where have you been all your life?'

Travis wanted to fuck his mother? In an instant Benny was back at primary school, pushed up against the back wall of the toilet block by Gavin Begley. He was grinning at Benny, his round face flushed. Behind them Gavin's gang cheered him on.

'Say it, bad boy! Say it!'

Benny gritted his teeth and tried not to think about the pain of Gavin pinning his arms against his sides. There was no way he was going to say it.

Gavin's foul breath was blowing in Benny's face. 'You know it's true. Everyone knows. Your mother fucked so many men she didn't even know who your father was.'

'He must have been a dumbass,' jeered one of the gang and they all laughed.

Before Benny knew what was happening, Gavin had him in a headlock. He was big for his age and his arms were like steel. He punched Benny in the side of the head. 'Say it!'

The gang took up the chorus again. 'Say it, Benny, say it!'

Benny was on the ground now, his face pushed into the dirt, with Gavin on top of him, pummelling him. He was crying and his nose was running, snot bubbling out on to his face. Gavin was going to kill him. He didn't want to die.

'My mother was a slut,' he mumbled into the ground.

Gavin took a handful of hair and yanked his head up. 'Can't hear you!'

Benny took a deep breath and said as loudly as he could, 'My mother was a slut.' Gavin let his head go and it thumped onto the ground. Benny's tears mingled with the dirt as he whispered so the others couldn't hear, 'I'm sorry, Mum, I'm sorry.'

'Let go!' Travis was gasping and spluttering. Benny had his hands around

Travis's throat and he was squeezing as tight as he could. He was powerful, unbeatable—Errol Flynn, Clint Eastwood and John Wayne all rolled into one.

Travis lunged out with his leg and kicked Benny in the balls. He felt the pain, but he didn't care. Mustering his newfound strength, he took one hand off Travis's throat and punched him hard in the stomach. Travis groaned and doubled over.

Benny shoved him on to the ground, jumped on top of him and pummelled him with every ounce of strength he had, just the way Gavin Begley had done all those years ago. And Tommy Rogers from next door and the police sergeant's son and that guy at the bus stop and all the others whose names he'd forgotten.

And it wasn't just those who had physically hurt him, it was anyone who had ever sneered at him and called him a retard. The girls who huddled in groups and giggled at him and called him a loser, the co-workers who hid his tools, stuck his head in the toilet and flushed it and made him eat tripe sandwiches. They were all here, like a ghostly army in his head and he was thrashing the shit out of every single one of them. And he couldn't stop, didn't want to stop.

'I'm sorry,' Travis gasped. 'I shouldn't have said that. Get off me.'

Benny punched him in the side of the head again. 'Say you're sorry for calling my mother a slut.'

'I didn't call her a slut.'

Benny punched him again.

'Okay, okay! I'm sorry for calling your mother a slut.'

'I want my money. And the gun. I know you've got them. You're just taking advantage of me because you think I'm stupid.'

'All right! Just stop, please!'

Benny stopped punching Travis and got off him. Travis rolled over and sat up. His face was bruised and bloody, his nose was squashed to one side of his face and one eye was shut. An angry red line circled his throat.

Travis looked at him warily out of his good eye. 'The money's in the car. I don't have the gun but I can tell you where to get it.'

'The gun was part of the deal,' Benny said.

'Yeah, well, I'm sorry,' Travis mumbled. Benny looked at him. Never did he think the day would come when Travis would apologise to him. But it meant nothing—Travis was only sorry because Benny had beaten him up.

'Go get the money,' he said.

Travis got to his feet, swaying a little, stopped for a minute to get his balance and stumbled to the front door. Benny followed him out to the car, just in case he tried to do a runner. Travis gingerly opened the boot, unscrewed the floor again and foraged around underneath, eventually drawing out a small zippered backpack.

Travis looked up at Leila's window. It was closed. 'We'd better do this inside.'

They went back inside and Benny watched as Travis sat on the couch and dug out bundles of fifty dollar notes. He counted out 20 bundles tied together with rubber bands and put them in a pile on the coffee table. 'That's twenty thousand.'

Benny picked one of the bundles and stared at it in wonderment. He'd never seen so much money before. He flipped through the notes just like he'd seen them do on TV.

'Are you sure it's twenty thousand?' he said.

'It's all there,' Travis said. 'There's a thousand in each bundle and there's twenty bundles.'

He would have to take Travis's word for it. It wasn't as if he could take it to the bank and ask them to count it for him.

'Have you got a pen and paper?' Travis asked. Benny went into the kitchenette and came back with a pen and a grocery store receipt.

Travis placed the receipt on the coffee table and wrote something on the back of it. He handed it to Benny. 'This is where you get the gun.'

On the paper was written in shaky letters 'Noel. 25 Garden St Petersham.'

'He doesn't do business over the phone,' Travis said, 'You have to go there.'

#

Benny was too hyped up to sleep. After Travis staggered out to his car, and drove off in a spray of gravel, Benny sat on the couch and looked at the bundles of notes, picking them up one by one, flipping through them, sniffing them. He even licked one; it tasted very bland.

He gathered them up, stashed ten bundles in his dirty clothes basket, wrapped the other ten bundles in a towel and stuffed it into his backpack. He had no idea how much a gun would cost, but he hoped he had enough. He picked up the piece of paper with the address on it, stuffed it into his shirt pocket, locked the front door and made his way to the bus stop.

He knew Petersham was not too far away, but reading the bus timetable was beyond him. It didn't take long for a bus to pull up. Benny allowed the two people waiting at the stop to get on, then poked his head in and said to the driver, 'Where can I catch the bus to Petersham?'

'From Livingstone Rd,' the driver said.

'Where's that?' Benny asked.

The driver gave an annoyed grunt. 'Ask Google Maps, buddy.'

A grey-haired woman sitting in the front seat leaned forward. 'Go to the end of this street, turn right and then right again.'

Benny thanked her. She smiled and waved at him as the bus moved off. Not being smart meant people often got fed up with him, but other times people helped him more than he asked for.

He found the bus stop in Livingstone Rd and boarded the next bus. He placed his backpack on his lap and hugged it close to him. He was nervous about carrying so much money with him. He glanced casually around at the other passengers. No one was even looking at him, let alone planning to steal his backpack, which, on the surface, was not much of a prize. It was old and faded and sported a large brown stain on the front where he'd spilt a chocolate milkshake on it.

He got off in the main street of Petersham. Delicious aromas wafted out from a nearby café, Harry's Joint, and he remembered he hadn't eaten breakfast. He went into the cafe, found a seat in the corner and when the waitress arrived he ordered the Big Breakfast. It was the most expensive dish on the menu, but what the hell! He could afford it now.

After eating everything on his plate right down to the last stalk of parsley, he left the café, found a quiet corner, got out his phone and asked Siri for directions to 25 Garden Street.

Following her directions, he found Garden St, a no-through street full of run-down cottages and scruffy front yards. There was no one around except for a small child at the far end riding a scooter up and down the road. A few beat-up cars hunched along the side of the road.

Number 25 was the worst. The front gate was rusted and hanging off its hinges, the lawn was knee high, the house sagged and the paint was peeling. It had an abandoned air, as if no one lived there. Had Travis given him the wrong address? On purpose?

The gate groaned as Benny opened it. He trod up the narrow concrete path almost hidden by the surrounding grass. He lifted the rusted door knocker and rapped. The sound rang out in the still morning air.

Nothing. He couldn't hear any movement in the house, so he rapped again. Instantly the door was flung open.

'I heard ya the first time,' a voice said. Benny stepped back at the sight before him. The man's face looked as if he'd spent his whole life in the sun. He had long, gray-white hair and a scraggy beard, and his jeans and shirt hung off his scrawny frame. He looked like one of the homeless men Benny had seen hanging around Hyde Park on the few occasions he'd ventured into the city.

'I'm looking for Noel,' Benny said.

The man's bright blue eyes, the only lively thing about him, bored into Benny. He said nothing.

'Maybe I've got the wrong address,' Benny stammered.

'Maybe you have,' the man said. 'Who are you?'

'Benny Goodchild. Travis gave me your address. He said you can get me…' He looked around. The neighbourhood was as deserted as before but he lowered his voice. 'A gun.'

'Did he now? And who the fuck is Travis?'

'Travis McDonald. He and I work at Lotus Flower Imports and Exports.'

The man continued to stare at him, and Benny was just starting to wonder if he had the wrong person, when the man opened the door wider and motioned him in.

Benny stepped inside into a short hallway. To his left was a living room with stained carpet, a mouldy couch and a small TV perched on an upside down plastic milk crate. On a low table in front of the couch stood an overflowing ashtray, a pile of empty pizza boxes and several empty bourbon and coke cans. The place reeked of stale cigarette smoke.

Noel—for now that he had invited Benny in, he assumed it was Noel— yanked Benny's backpack from him, grabbed him by the arm and pushed him up against the wall of the hallway. 'Spread your legs and put your arms up against the wall.'

Benny did as he was told. Noel patted him all over from top to bottom. 'What are you doing?' Benny said.

'Checking you for wires. You don't look like a cop but these days you can't tell.'

When he'd finished, Benny turned around in time to see Noel opening his backpack. He pulled out the towel, unwrapped it and whistled as the bundles of money rolled out on to the floor.

'There's a lot of dough here. What did you do? Rob a bank?'

'No.'

'You shouldn't walk round with it, it's dangerous. What if you got mugged?'

A cold chill gripped Benny. Was Noel going to steal his money?

He thought quickly. Noel was old and skinny and if Benny caught him by surprise… He aimed a fist at Noel's jaw. But Noel got in first, hitting Benny on the cheek and causing him to reel backwards, hitting his head against the wall. Benny put his hand to his stinging cheek. Noel was grinning at him.

'I might be old, mate, but I'm still quick on my feet.'

He nodded towards the money. 'I'm not going to take your dosh.'

Keeping a wary eye on Noel, Benny bent over and picked up the towel and the bundles of money and stuffed them back into his backpack. He put his hand to his cheek. It felt hot and swollen.

'Now that we've established you're not a cop, I need to know what you want the gun for,' Noel said.

'Why?'

'I'm what they call a responsible vendor, mate. You ask anyone who knows me and they'll all tell you the same thing. 'Noel is a responsible guy.' I have to make sure that selling you a gun is not going to harm the community.'

What did he mean by not harming the community? As far as Benny could see, killing Lucas would only benefit the community, as well as Olivia—one less bully. Olivia probably wasn't the only person Lucas was nasty to. Of course, Lucas's mum and dad wouldn't be happy. Or his brothers and sisters, if he had any. Or his friends. But this was Olivia's life at stake. Benny had seen it on the news so many times—women being killed by their husbands after years of domestic violence. A life taken for a life saved. It all evened out.

'I'm going to kill Lucas,' Benny said. 'He's Olivia's ex-husband and he beats her up. Olivia's my girlfriend,' he added. 'We're going to London and then we'll get married.'

It wasn't true—yet. But he didn't care about lying to Noel, as his gut feeling told him that Noel was no stranger to telling lies himself.

In an instant, Noel grabbed Benny's arms and pinned them up against his back.

'Promise me you're telling the truth,' he commanded. He gripped harder and pain shot through Benny's arms. 'Yes, it's the truth,' he gasped.

Noel released his grip and Benny rubbed his arms and shoulders.

'You'd better be telling me the truth,' Noel said. 'If I find out that you've done one of those mass shootings like they do in America and killed innocent people, I'll come after you and shoot you myself, if the cops haven't.'

'I already told you, it's the truth.'

'Ok, buddy. This Lucas sounds like a bad dude. Beating up women is lower than a snake's belly. I've done a lot of bad things in my time, but I've never laid a finger on a woman. Except to root 'em.' He grinned. 'So, what sort of weapon were you thinking of…what's your name?'

'Benny.' Damn, he should have given a false name. 'I don't know.'

'You don't know much, do you? I think it would be a safe bet that you've never used one.'

Benny nodded, then realising that Noel might think he was saying that yes, he had used a gun, shook his head.

'So, young Benny, if I were to sell you a gun, say a nice little 9mm Browning, how would you know how to fire it?'

Benny hadn't thought that far ahead. Getting the gun was the hard part, he'd worry about how to use it when he had it. But Noel wanted an answer now.

'I'd learn it on YouTube.'

Noel let out a hearty guffaw. 'That's the best one I've heard yet.' He shook his head. 'You kids live your whole lives on YouTube. You probably learn how to fuck on YouTube.'

Benny squirmed inside at the thought of watching people have sex on the screen. 'No, I haven't,' he said.

Noel slapped him on the shoulder. 'Just having a lend, mate. I'll do you a deal. It's five grand for the gun and for an extra grand I'll throw in a lesson on how to use it.'

Benny gaped at Noel. Five thousand for the gun was one thing, but a thousand dollars for one lesson?

'Take it from me, mate,' Noel said. 'One lesson from me will equal ten lessons on YouTube. I've got a property out the back of Dural. I'll take you out there and give you some hands-on training. I'd hate to see you botch this job because you shot your own foot off instead of the wife beater.'

He had no choice but to accept Noel's offer. He drew out six bundles of notes from his backpack and handed them to Noel. Noel flicked through them, counting under his breath, then disappeared down the hallway. He returned with an old rag and a large straw hat.

'Let's go. No time like the present.'

CHAPTER 15

Noel locked the front door and led Benny to a beat-up old Mazda parked on side of the road a few doors down. He got in, reached over and unlocked the passenger door. Benny slid into the seat and Noel leaned over, the rag in his hand. 'Turn your head, I'm going to blindfold you.'

'Why?' Benny said. But as soon as he'd spoken, the rag was over his eyes and tied at the back. It smelt of grease and stale body odour.

'I don't want you knowing where this place is. And give me your mobile phone.'

Benny reached into his pocket and gave Noel his mobile phone. 'What are you doing with it?'

'For a smart guy you ask a lot of questions.'

Smart guy. Was he serious? He knew that people often said the exact opposite of what they meant, so maybe Noel was really saying he was dumb.

'I'm checking it for GPS tracking apps.'

'I wouldn't even know how to get one,' Benny said.

'I'll keep it for the time being, anyway. Slump down in your seat and put this hat over your face and pretend to be asleep.' Benny felt the hat land in his lap and did as he was told.

'I have to ask one more question,' Benny said. 'How long will it take to get there?'

'Not long, about 45 minutes.'

Forty-five minutes seemed to take forever. Life was pretty boring when you were blindfolded. Benny took his mind to London—or how he imagined

London from what he'd seen on TV. Tall buildings, the big clock—what was it called?—Big Ben, the bustling crowds, the endless traffic and screeching horns.

Then he saw himself in a pub like those he'd seen on the British crime shows—cosy, with a fireplace, Olivia by his side, her face glowing in the candlelight. She was sipping on a glass of wine; Benny had a Coke. Make that diet Coke. They were enjoying a pre-dinner drink before going to the theatre, Olivia looking like an angel in a gown that sparkled and shimmered and showed off her curves, and Benny in a suit and bow tie. He'd never worn a suit in his life, not even to Auntie Rose and Auntie Fran's funerals. He made a mental note to go shopping when he returned from Noel's place. He'd have to have a nap first though…

Someone was shaking him on the shoulder. 'Wake up, kid.' He opened his eyes, still in darkness, and then remembered. Noel whipped the hat off his face and untied the blindfold.

They were parked in front of another run-down cottage, with a small mown patch in front and a vast expanse of bush marching in on it from all sides. At the back of the house was a large shed filled with old machinery. What Benny noticed the most was the silence. It was deafening.

'Walk this way,' Noel said. He led Benny around the side of the house to the shed. They wended their way through huge hulks of machinery, a car body, two rusted pushbikes and piles of metal bits and pieces. Was that a snake slithering away into the dark corner? Benny shivered and pretended not to see it. He didn't want Noel to think he was scared.

Noel opened a door at the end of the shed and they entered another room. The floor was covered with thick carpet and the walls were lined with a strange material that looked like a lot of tiny pyramids all joined together. Benny couldn't help running his fingers over it.

'Acoustic foam,' Noel said. 'Soundproofs the room. Don't want any nosy neighbours dropping by.'

On the back wall, were a number of targets of different sizes—the normal circular target with its bullseye, a flock of ducks, various wild animals and several of the prime minister, a big grin on his moon face and a bullseye on his chest.

In the far corner of the room was another door with a padlock on it. Noel unlocked it and went inside. Benny hovered at the doorway. The walls were lined with racks of guns of all shapes and sizes. Benny imagined them all going off at once in a deafening explosion of gunfire. Noel brought over a slim, brown gun; in his other hand was a long metal tube.

'This is the 9mm Browning. Unless you're popping it off in the middle of nowhere, you'll need a silencer as well.' He held up the tube in his hand and Benny nodded.

'We'll start without the silencer to get you used to it. There are three things you have to remember. First, always act as if it's loaded, even when it's not. Secondly, keep it pointed in a safe direction at all times, away from yourself. You wouldn't believe the number of people who've shot their toes off because the gun went off when it was aimed at the ground. And thirdly, keep your finger well away from the trigger until you're ready to shoot. You understand?'

Benny nodded. He was concentrating hard to remember it all. What would it be like to have no toes? It would be hard to balance. Wouldn't you fall over all the time?

Noel showed him how to load the gun, then gave it to him to try. He'd never held a gun, and it was heavier than he expected. He had to load it a number of times before he could do it easily. Then Noel showed him to hold the gun with two hands—easier to control the recoil, he said. He showed him the correct stance—knees lightly bent, feet shoulder-width apart—how to sight it and finally, how to aim it at the target. Then it was time to shoot.

'Squeeze the trigger and keep squeezing it until it shoots,' Noel said. Benny did as he was told, aiming it at the prime minister's chest. It seemed as if the bullet would never release, and then it did. Benny jumped back; he was surprised at the force of it. The bullet went through the prime minister's eye.

Noel applauded. 'I always reckoned he was one-eyed.' Benny tried a few more times and on the sixth attempt he got the prime minister smack in the chest.

'You're not bad for a first timer,' Noel said. 'I think you've got a natural ability.'

Natural ability. A thrill ran through Benny. No one had ever told him he had a natural ability. Except Auntie Vi, who said he had a natural ability to attract trouble.

'Repeat after me,' Noel said. 'Point, relax, squeeze. That's your mantra.'

'Point, relax, squeeze,' Benny said.

Noel handed him another case of bullets. 'Here, shoot another round.'

#

Benny moved over to the window seat on the bus to allow room for the fat woman with all her shopping bags to sit next to him. He wedged his backpack in between his feet.

Noel's parting words were still ringing in his ears. 'Good luck, buddy. And if the cops get you, don't mention my name. If you do, I'll hear about it and then ....' He made the shape of a gun with his hands, pointing it at Benny.

The woman was huffing and puffing with the effort of heaving herself and her bags into the seat. She looked at Benny and her glance fell upon the backpack. Benny broke out in a sweat. He not only had money in it but a gun. Maybe she had X-ray vision like Superman and could see inside his backpack. He told himself of course she didn't, Superman wasn't real. But she was giving him strange looks. Or was it just his imagination?

Benny got off at the next stop and let Siri guide him the rest of the way home. As he walked down his front driveway, the curtains fluttered in the upstairs window. Leila was spying on him again. As soon as he got inside, there was a knock on his back door. 'Benny can I talk to you?'

'I can't,' Benny yelled back. 'I have to sleep before I go to work.'

'Please Benny! Just for a minute.'

She sounded distressed. What was wrong this time? The lid on the Vegemite jar again?

Benny opened the door. Leila's thin cheeks were tear-stained and she threw herself into his arms, sobbing uncontrollably.

'What's happened?' Benny asked, alarmed. No one could get that upset over a Vegemite jar.

He waited until her sobs died down. She raised her sodden face. 'My cancer's come back. It's in my bones. The doctor said I'll be lucky to make two years.'

Benny patted her back awkwardly. 'The doctors told my Auntie Fran she only had six months to live. And she lived for two more years.'

He hoped that would cheer her up, but she just broke out into a fresh bout of sobbing. 'So what?' she said in between sobs. 'That doesn't mean it's going to happen to me.'

She pressed her body into Benny. He felt every part of it through her thin cotton pants and blouse, her breasts squashed against him and her crotch jammed up against his. He gently disentangled himself from her. 'Do you want me to make you a cup of tea?'

Leila shook her head. 'I just want you to hold me, to make love to me. It would make me so happy, God knows I haven't got much happiness left in my life now.'

Benny looked away from her pleading eyes. 'I can't Leila, I've already told you that.'

'Can't you forget about your girlfriend for a little while? She doesn't need you right now as much as I do.'

That wasn't true. Leila didn't have a jealous ex-husband trying to kill her. If Benny didn't save Olivia, she could well die before Leila. But he couldn't tell Leila that.

'I can't forget about Olivia. And I can't make love to you, it wouldn't be right.'

Added to the fact that she'd called him a retard. It still hurt every time he thought about it.

Leila put her arms around his neck and kissed him full on the lips. She picked up his hand and placed it on her breast.

'Don't forget, Benny, who owns this house.'

He took his hand away from her breast. 'I know you own this house. You don't have to keep reminding me.'

'I can ask you to leave. Any time. Tomorrow if need be.'

Something told him, that gut feeling again, that Leila would never throw him out. She needed him, even if he didn't make love to her, because she had no one else. And little did she know he'd be gone very soon, thousands of miles away, and she'd be left to die alone. He felt sad and guilty and mean all at the same time. It was horrible for Leila, but it was Olivia he loved. He had to stay strong. For her.

He shook his head. 'I'm sorry.' Before she could respond, he went inside and closed the door.

CHAPTER 16

Travis arrived at work sporting a huge black eye and bruises on his face and neck.

'What happened to you?' Ned asked.

'Walked into a door, mate,' Travis said. But he grinned as he said it, as if it were a joke and Ned grinned back, as if he were in on the joke.

Benny felt a swell of pride that he had caused these injuries. And oddly, Travis wasn't angry at him. In fact, it was the opposite—Travis was more respectful towards him and for the first time ever he worked an entire shift without making fun of Benny.

Mick was still absent, and Ned had called in Leon, one of the day workers, to do an extra shift. At tea break, Benny caught up with Travis. 'When are you coming to get the bag?'

'Be patient, mate. Mick's in the clink. The cops picked him up on an old warrant, but the judge refused him bail. He got word to me to be careful— he thinks the cops are watching me because they know we're mates.'

Frustration was eating at Benny. He wanted to get the money from this stash before he went to London. He was sure he had enough already for the flight over and accommodation, but the more money he had, the easier it would be to treat Olivia in the way she deserved—buy her beautiful clothes, take her out to dinner and the theatre, to Paris for the weekend and Spain for the summer holidays. According to Auntie Rose, Mallorca, an island in Spain, was the romance capital of the world.

Travis gave him a friendly pat on the shoulder. 'Hey, I want the money just as much as you do. I'll arrange for a mate to come and pick it up. Gotta find someone I can trust not to do the dirty on me. I'll keep you posted.'

#

When he got home from work, Benny had a quick breakfast and crashed into bed. He was exhausted as he'd only slept a couple of hours the previous day, and it was after midday before he woke up.

He pulled the backpack out of the top of his cupboard where he'd hidden it under a couple of towels. Not that it was a very good hiding place—if the police came knocking on the door and searched his flat, they wouldn't take long to find it. He'd have a hard time explaining it along with the stash of drugs. But they had no reason to visit him, and as soon as he'd finished with the gun, he'd throw it in the harbour. He could only hope that Travis's mate would come soon for the drugs.

He took out the gun and examined it from all angles, running his fingers along its smooth edges. He fitted the silencer on, gripped it the way Noel had taught him and aimed it at the wardrobe door. It had taken him a while to get used to the silencer; it made the gun heavier and dragged it downwards, and he had to be extra careful with his aim.

'You're dead, Lucas Bartlett!' Benny said as he squeezed the trigger. The gun clicked. Of course, he hadn't put any bullets in. 'Don't play around with it, even when it's got no bullets,' Noel had told him. 'It's a dangerous habit.'

But Benny couldn't resist it. While he had the gun in his hand, he was in charge and people had to do what he commanded. No one could bully him. It was a delicious feeling.

'Apologise for everything you've done to Olivia,' Benny said, aiming his gun at an imaginary Lucas. 'No, that's not good enough. Say it like you mean it, or you're dead meat.'

He listened for Lucas's imaginary response. 'That's better. But I'm sorry to say I lied. I'm going to kill you anyway.' He squeezed the trigger and imagined the bullet hitting Lucas in the chest, killing him instantly. He hoped he could kill him with the first shot, but Noel had said to be prepared to put two or three bullets in him to make sure he was dead.

He had to do this quickly. While he was feeling brave. In two nights it was his rostered night off. He would do it then. Meanwhile he had some shopping to do.

CHAPTER 17

Leila was looking out her window as Benny got out of the taxi. She seemed to spend an awful lot of time looking out into the wide open world that she was too scared to be a part of.

She gave a low whistle. He was wearing the suit, shirt and tie he'd bought at Harrolds in the city, as well as the shiny black shoes to go with them. The pants were too long, but for an extra $50 they'd altered them for him while he went into the trendy cafe next door and ordered a green smoothie. To his surprise, he rather liked it.

When he returned to collect the suit, he went into the change rooms, put it on and stuffed his jeans and shirt in the Harrolds bag. After all, he was treating himself to lunch in a posh restaurant, so he had to look the part.

He took out his wallet and looked at the taxi meter. Fifty-two dollars. He handed two fifty dollar notes to the taxi driver. 'Keep the change.'

He'd always wanted to say that to a cab driver, just like people did in movies. Not that he was in the habit of taking cabs, but he'd allowed himself the extravagance this time because it was easier than trying to juggle all his packages on the bus.

'Gee, thanks mate,' the taxi driver said. He opened the boot, jumped out and helped Benny out with his shopping bags.

'Who died and left you money?' Leila called out. Benny hadn't thought about explaining how he'd come into money, but Leila had given him the perfect cue.

'My Auntie Vi,' he called back. She was his only living relative and she'd been in the nursing home for years. For all he knew she could be dead, though he didn't think she had very much money. But Leila wasn't to know that.

He went inside and dropped all his parcels on the living room floor. He stood in front of the mirror in the bedroom and took another look at himself. The suit, in charcoal grey, made him look slimmer and fitted as if it were made for him. He'd pretended to be a businessman about town as he sat in the restaurant of the Grand Pacific Hotel, eating his rump steak with garlic mash, braised Asian vegetables and some sort of jus, which turned out to be a fancy name for sauce. It was the only dish on the menu he could (mostly) understand.

In between mouthfuls he checked his phone, as if he were reading important messages. No one took a second look at him; they were all too engrossed in their own conversations. Auntie Fran's advice echoed in his head. 'Act as if you're as good as everyone else. Because you are.'

It was fine sitting in an air-conditioned restaurant and taxi, but now in his sweatbox of a flat, he didn't feel so stylish. He shed the suit and put on his baggy shorts and T-shirt. His body gave a sigh of relief.

He went back into the living room and opened his packages. It was like Christmas, even though he knew what was in them, but sad because there was no one else to enjoy it with him. There were half a dozen shirts, a couple more ties, new jeans and a pair of Nike sneakers.

In the next bundle of packages he opened a small case and took out a diamond bracelet. He didn't know much about jewellery, but he knew that women liked diamonds. At least that's what Auntie Rose always said when she came back from one of her overseas trips flashing the rings and necklaces that her latest boyfriend had bought her.

He was looking in the window of the jewellers shop when he saw the bracelet—delicate silver with a dangling heart, inside of which nestled three diamonds. So dainty, it would look perfect on Olivia's tiny wrist. He stared in the front window for so long trying to pluck up the courage to go in, that the sales attendant, an oily man with slicked back hair and a huge moustache, came outside.

This was earlier in the morning, before Benny had bought the suit, so he was still in his jeans and shirt. The man looked him up and down. 'Can I help you, sir?' It was clear from his tone of voice that he thought Benny was beyond any sort of help he could give him.

Benny pointed to the bracelet. 'I'll have that one.'

The corners of the man's plump lips turned up. 'That bracelet is $2500. Sir,' he added.

That was a lot of money. But Benny had plenty of money left and Olivia was worth every cent. And more.

He nodded. 'Okay.'

The man gave him a curious look and motioned for him to come inside. He unlocked the window, took the bracelet off the stand and held it up so it sparkled under the light.

'The diamonds are from South Africa, and the bracelet was hand-crafted in Italy by Lorenzo Flavio, one of the world's most renowned craftsmen.'

Benny nodded. 'Okay.'

The man looked at him like the teachers at school had when he'd answered a question and got it wrong. Which had happened a lot.

'Would you like to have a closer look at it?'

'No.'

The man waited as if expecting Benny to say more, but when he didn't, he went behind the counter, brought out a case from under it and nestled the bracelet into it. 'Will that be credit, sir?'

'Cash, please.' Benny got out his wallet and started pulling out the notes, one by one until he thought he had enough. 'I've lost count. Is that enough?'

'You've given me one too many,' the man said, handing back a fifty dollar note. He might be treating Benny as if he was a piece of dog shit on his shoe, but at least he didn't rip him off.

Benny held the bracelet in his hand as if it were a small, fragile animal. The diamond heart twinkled at him. If only Auntie Rose could see him now—she would never have believed he could afford to buy something so beautiful. He imagined the look on Olivia's face when he presented it to her and she opened the case, and the gasps of surprise and delight. Benny would fasten it on her wrist for her, and she'd throw her arms around him and exclaim that it was the best present she'd ever received.

He placed the bracelet back in its case and fished out another small package. It was a necklace with a ruby pendant, a present for Leila; red was her favourite colour. It cost nowhere near $2500, he didn't want to spend that much on her, but he wanted to buy her something to cheer her up. He went to a different jewellery shop to buy that one, where the attendant, a young girl, was very nice to him.

He put the necklace back in its box, went up the interior staircase and knocked on the door. The door opened and Leila's face lit up. Benny realised it was the first time that he'd gone up of his own accord, rather than at her invitation. Benny thrust the package at her.

'Ooh, what's this?'

'A present.'

'You're a master of the obvious.' She looked at the box and then at him. 'Why?'

Benny shrugged and looked down at his feet. 'Just to make you feel better.'

Leila opened the box and drew out the necklace. 'Ooh, it's beautiful! How did you know that rubies are my favourite stones?' She placed it around her neck and turned around. 'Would you be an angel?'

The clasp was tiny and Benny's fingers felt big and clumsy as he fastened it. It was an uncomfortably intimate thing to do; something a husband would do for his wife, and he imagined it was Olivia's graceful neck he was putting it around instead of Leila's wrinkled neck.

He had to admit, though, the necklace suited Leila, the red of the ruby brightening her sallow features. Her eyes were shiny—were those tears?

'Is that true about your aunt leaving you the money?'

Benny nodded and tried to think of something else so he wouldn't look guilty about lying. He studied the glass of champagne on the kitchen bench, watching the bubbles floating up to the surface.

'I have a reputation to maintain, so I won't stand for anything that's not above board. I don't want the police turning up on my doorstep and giving the neighbours something else to gossip about.'

'Okay,' Benny said. He met her gaze because he knew if he didn't, it would look suspicious.

'I didn't like the look of your friend the other day. Jason.'

Benny looked puzzled. 'Oh, you mean Travis.' As soon as he said it, he remembered that Travis had introduced himself as Jason.

'He told me his name was Jason,' Leila said.

'He likes that name better,' Benny said. Leila was looking at him with pursed lips. He crossed his fingers behind his back. 'There's nothing wrong with him, he's a law-abiding citizen.' Clint Eastwood had used that phrase in one of his movies and Benny had made a point of remembering it because it sounded impressive. It was more impressive when Clint said it, though.

'I hope so,' Leila said. She fingered the ruby, then said, 'Would you like to stay for a drink? I've got ginger beer.'

'No, thank-you. I've got some things to do.'

'Are you seeing your girlfriend tonight? What's her name? Angela?'

'Olivia. No, I'm not seeing her tonight.' He'd done enough lying for one day. 'But I will be soon.'

#

All was quiet at 125 Greygum Ave. It was 9.30 p.m. and all the windows were dark. A light was on over the front porch. In the dim street lighting Benny couldn't see Lucas's car parked anywhere on the street. All the other houses were still and silent. A typical suburban street on a Wednesday night. Why wasn't Lucas home?

Benny was sweating. He had bought a jacket with deep pockets to carry the gun and even though it was now early autumn, the nights were still warm. And he'd walked the five kilometres from his house to Lucas's—less risky than catching a bus or riding his bike. The fewer people he met along the way the better.

He looked around for somewhere to hide until Lucas came home. There was nowhere; only the large plane tree at the end of the street where he'd loitered the first time he'd visited. But that was during the day—a person hanging around there at night would look suspicious to anyone driving down the street.

Lucas's front yard was bare—no trees or bushes. Perhaps there was somewhere at the back of the house where he could hide. Then a frightening thought occurred to him. What if Lucas was at Olivia's house? And what if he was attacking her? And this time he killed her? He had to go there now. If Lucas wasn't there, by the time Benny arrived back here, he might be home.

Benny walked back to the shopping centre at Newtown and hailed a cab. It was the quickest way to Olivia's house. He pulled his cap down over his forehead and looked out the passenger window, so the driver couldn't see his face. Benny asked him to let him off a couple of streets early. 'Keep the change, Buddy,' he said, handing the driver a fifty dollar note.

He ran the remaining two blocks, panting and sweating by the time he arrived. His heart gave a leap when he spotted Lucas's car parked a little way up the street under a street lamp. He crept to his usual spot in the bushes under the kitchen window, and drew his loaded gun out of his jacket pocket. He attached the silencer and peeked through the kitchen window.

The kitchen was empty, but voices floated out from the living room.

'So you were just intending to jet off to London forever and not tell me?'

'It's none of your business what I do. How did you find out?'

'Never you mind. Suffice it to say you have at least one workmate who is happy to give away all your secrets.'

'Lucas, this is nothing to do with you. You're not even supposed to be here unless you get permission from me first. That's part of the AVO.'

'I don't care about the fucking AVO, it's just a piece of paper. I don't have to get permission from anyone to talk to my own wife. And don't go on about not being my wife. We're not divorced, so as far as I'm concerned you're still my wife.'

Olivia suddenly appeared in the kitchen, swiping her phone from the bench. So she'd bought a new phone. Not that it did her much good—Lucas was behind her, grabbed her and bent her arm back. Olivia squealed in pain and dropped the phone on the floor. She let out an ear-splitting scream. 'Help!'

Lucas gripped her around the neck in a choke-hold. 'Shut up, bitch!'

Olivia gave a swift kick back and got Lucas in the crotch. He howled in pain, and loosened his grip just enough for Olivia to escape from his hold. He lunged at her and threw her to the ground.

Benny had seen enough. He dashed out of the bushes, gun in hand, around the side of the house to the front door. It was unlocked. He flung it open and raced into the kitchen. Olivia was now lying on the floor, Lucas on top of her, his hands around her throat. She was making strange gurgling sounds. When she saw Benny, surprise and terror flashed in her eyes.

Benny aimed the gun at the middle of Lucas's back. His aim had to be perfect, so that he didn't shoot Olivia as well. He released the safety and gripped the gun the way Noel had taught him. Point, Relax, Squeeze. As if sensing his presence, Lucas swung around. His eyes widened as he saw the gun. He took his hands off Olivia's throat and lunged at the gun.

But Benny was already squeezing the trigger. The gun went off and Lucas pitched back on top of Olivia, blood soaking his shirt.

CHAPTER 18

Olivia scrambled out from under Lucas, coughing and gasping. Benny watched her, helpless, not knowing what to do. Lucas was sprawled on his back on the floor, mouth ajar, eyes still open in shock. His shirt was covered in blood. Benny looked away—all that blood was making him feel sick.

Olivia got her breath back and looked at him. Her clothes were blood spattered where Lucas had fallen on top of her. Her hair was a mess, her neck was red and already starting to bruise and one side of her face was swollen, as if Lucas had hit her. Benny longed to take her in his arms and kiss away all the hurt, inside and outside.

'Why did you do that?' Olivia croaked.

'He was going to kill you.'

She looked over at Lucas, shuddered, then back at Benny. Her eyes were glassy; she started to shiver. Benny dropped his gun, went into her bedroom and whipped the quilt off her bed. He dragged it out and wrapped it tenderly around her shoulders.

She was still shivering, seemingly unaware of the quilt draped around her. 'What are you doing here?' she whispered.

'I'm saving you.' The words came tumbling out, the words he'd wanted to say to her for so long. 'I love you, it makes me so unhappy when I see him hurting you. I want to help you get away from him.'

She hadn't taken her eyes off him. 'When have you seen him hurting me?'

Benny met her gaze. He wouldn't lie to her; she deserved the truth. But before he could open his mouth, Olivia's eyes cleared and a look of understanding dawned on her face. 'You've been stalking me, haven't you?'

'No. I've been hiding outside your kitchen window. To protect you. If I hadn't been here tonight, you might be dead.'

The image of his beloved Olivia as a lifeless body on the floor almost wrenched his heart out of his chest. He watched her as she sat there with her hands over her face. Was she crying?

When she looked up there were no tears, but her face was deathly white. 'So that's why you were in the area the other night when you knocked on the door. You'd been spying on us.'

'I wasn't spying,' Benny said. 'I was looking after you.' His voice trembled. 'Please believe me.'

Olivia shook her head. 'You don't get it, do you? I trusted you and you turned out be nothing more than a creepy pervert.'

Benny couldn't believe what he was hearing. His sweet, angelic Olivia had called him a pervert. That was worse than retard.

Brakes screeched. Car doors slammed. Someone hammered on the front door. 'Police, open up!'

Olivia and Benny looked in the direction of the door. Neither moved. The door burst open and a troupe of policemen charged in.

The first cop in whipped out his gun and pointed it at Benny.

'Put your hands up!'

#

Three days later. Sydney Morning Herald.

A man has been charged with murder following a shooting in Marrickville last Wednesday night. Benjamin Owen Goodchild, 42, appeared in Newtown Local Court yesterday, charged with the murder of 36-year-old Lucas Bartlett. It is understood that Mr Goodchild knew Mr Bartlett's estranged wife Olivia.

Neighbour Doris Crawley, who heard screaming at the residence and called the police, said, 'As the police were taking him away, he was yelling out, 'I love you, Olivia! I did it for you! I saved your life!'

Mr Goodchild was also charged with Possession of a dangerous drug after 2.5 kilograms of heroin was found in his home. His landlady Mrs Leila Murphy, who was present at court, said, 'I suspected he was up to no good. He was hanging around with some unsavoury characters and splashing a lot of money around. So after I reported it to police I wasn't surprised when they found the drugs. But killing that man, that was a shock. I'm an agoraphobic and I've got terminal cancer but I had to come to court to see for myself. Poor Benny, he's a bit simple, so I guess you never can tell.'

It is understood that Mr Goodchild is intellectually impaired. He entered no plea and was remanded in custody to appear in court again in a month's time, and also ordered to undergo assessment. Further drug charges are pending.'

18 months later. Sydney Morning Herald.

An intellectually disabled man was sentenced to six years imprisonment, with a non-parole period of three years, for manslaughter yesterday in Sydney District Court. Benjamin Goodchild, 43, was charged with the manslaughter, downgraded from murder, of Lucas Bartlett, 36, at Newtown in western Sydney on 6 March last year.

The court heard that Mr Goodchild was the gardener of Mr Bartlett's estranged wife Olivia and had become obsessed with her. He claimed he obtained a gun with the purpose of threatening Mr Bartlett, because he had been assaulting Mrs Bartlett, but he had no intention of killing Mr Bartlett. When Mr Goodchild arrived at Mrs Bartlett's home on the night in question and discovered Mr Bartlett assaulting her, he fired his gun, intending only to frighten him, instead shooting him in the chest and killing him.

Mr Goodchild said that he was in love with Mrs Bartlett and only wanted to save her life.

'He was a pervert, I had no idea he'd been stalking me,' Mrs Bartlett, who now resides in London, said. When asked to comment on Mr Goodchild's sentence, she said, 'It's a joke! Six years for a man's life! My husband had his faults but he didn't deserve to die. But now I just

want to get on with my life and forget that Benjamin Goodchild ever existed.'

Mr Goodchild was also convicted of Possessing dangerous drugs and sentenced to 12 months imprisonment, to be served concurrently. Charges of Stalking and Trafficking dangerous drugs were previously dropped. Taking into account pre-sentence custody, Mr Goodchild will be eligible for parole in March 2019.

CHAPTER 19

May 2019.

The bus jerked to a stop. Three passengers got on. The last was a beefy man in his thirties—tattooed arms, a greasy, acne-scarred face and a black cap inscribed with 'Anarchy' in large red letters, beside two fingers making a rude gesture.

Benny quickly looked out the window, heart racing. But it was too late; the man had seen him. He made a beeline for Benny and sat down beside him. The bus rumbled out into the traffic.

'Fancy seein' you here, bad boy,' he said. 'When did you get out?'

Rodney had been two cells down from Benny in the Additional Support Unit in Long Bay Correctional Centre, which housed prisoners with intellectual disabilities. Benny soon found out after being transferred there that people with intellectual disabilities could be just as nasty and frightening as the rest of the prison population—Rodney being one of them.

'A few weeks ago,' Benny said.

'How come they let a retard like you out?'

Benny took a deep breath, closed his eyes and began his special technique. While in prison he'd finally worked out how to do what Auntie Fran had suggested—grow an inner shell. He imagined he had grown a hard shell all around his heart, which was like a little crab hidden inside. When someone said something mean, he imagined the words hitting the shell and bouncing off again. So they no longer had the power to hurt him. But he had to concentrate very hard for it to work.

Rodney nudged him in the ribs. 'I asked you a question.'

'I got out on parole.'

'Whose dick did you have to suck?'

'No one's.'

Benny looked out the window again, fervently hoping that Rodney wouldn't be getting out at his stop. In prison he told anyone who listened that he had ADHD, as if it were something to be proud of. Benny didn't know what ADHD was—all he knew was that Rodney could blow his top in an instant at the smallest thing, which made Benny very wary of him.

Rodney pulled out his mobile phone and earplugs from his jeans pocket, connected them and started jiggling his legs to the music. Benny continued to gaze out the window. Three years in jail had crawled; he had felt as if he was in there forever. And now the dazzling blue sky, the warm sunlight, the fiery autumn leaves of the maple trees, the traffic and pedestrians, everything that had just been in the background before he went to prison, now shone with a special light.

Rodney nudged him again. 'Where'd you go today?'

'I went to see my old boss, to see if I could get a job.'

'At the sheltered workshop?' He sniggered.

Benny didn't answer. Concentrate, shell, bounce words off.

'Why don't you ask me where I went today?' Rodney said.

That was the last thing Benny cared about, but he didn't want Rodney to get angry with him here on the bus.

'Where did you go today?'

'I went to Kings Cross and had a root. Crystal—big tits and tight pussy. I can give you her phone number if you want.'

Benny's stomach roiled in embarrassment. 'It's okay, thanks.'

'Your loss, mate.'

Rodney jiggled his legs and nodded his head to the beat for another couple of stops. As the bus screeched to a halt outside the shopping centre, he got up and slapped Benny on the shoulder. 'See you round, bad boy. Don't kill anyone.'

The two young girls sitting in front of him also stood up to get off the bus.

They turned and looked at Benny, then at each other and giggled as they followed Rodney off the bus. Benny slumped down in his seat. His relief at Rodney going was diluted by his humiliation that the two girls had probably heard everything he said.

It was five o'clock by the time he arrived back at the house he shared with three other intellectually disabled residents. Cecilia, his support worker, was sitting at the dining table tapping away on her laptop.

She looked up at him and smiled. His heart did a somersault. The shape of her face and her curly brown hair reminded him of his mother. Cecelia was his friend; his only friend at the moment. He didn't much like his parole officer, who was a crusty old bag, but it was Cecelia who'd helped him the most. She picked him up from prison on his release day, took him to the donut shop, his first port of call, and then to buy new clothes and a new DVD player.

'How are you, Benny?' she said. 'Did you have a good day?'

'Yes, thank you.'

She nodded towards the kitchen. 'You do what you have to do. I'm finishing this report.'

It was Benny's turn, along with Lillian, to cook the dinner. He roused Lillian, a heavyset girl in her twenties, from the couch in front of the TV, and supervised her while she peeled the potatoes and put them in a saucepan on the stove to boil.

As soon as his back was turned to get out the frying pan, Lillian wandered back to the living room. 'Lillian, you have to watch the potatoes, otherwise they'll burn,' Benny called out.

She waddled back, looking at him uncertainly from under heavy-lidded eyes. Benny indicated the oven timer. 'Turn this around to here.' He pointed to half way between five and ten minutes.

She stretched out a pudgy arm and turned the dial.

'Stop right there. Now press it.'

She did so. 'Good girl. When the alarm rings, you press the button again to stop it, and then you take the potatoes off the stove. You understand?'

Lillian nodded and looked down, twisting her hands. 'Can I go and watch Scooby-Doo now?'

'Okay, don't have it up too loud so you can hear the alarm.'

Lillian scurried back into the living room. Benny put the lamb chops on to cook in the frying pan and they were soon sizzling away, making his stomach rumble. He closed the lid and went to sit at the table next to Cecilia.

She looked up. 'You're doing well with Lillian.'

Benny gave a modest shrug. 'When it's our turn to cook, I always do most of it.'

'She's learning, though, that's the main thing.'

She closed her laptop. 'It's been two months now since your release from prison. Are you all settled in?'

Benny considered for a few moments. 'I guess.'

It was one of the conditions of his parole that he reside in a supervised disability share house. He couldn't see the sense in it; after all, he'd lived on his own for years before. Why did he need supervision now? But he also didn't want to stay a moment longer in jail than he had to, and if that was the price of freedom, he would pay it.

When Cecilia suggested that he help look after the other residents, it had made the situation more enjoyable. He was happy to help them and teach them new things. But he didn't want to stay here forever.

'I know you'd be happier if you were working,' she said. 'Did you see your old boss at Lotus Flower today?'

'Yes.' Ned had welcomed him back like a long-lost friend and invited him for a cup of coffee. It made Benny feel bad about deceiving him with Travis and Mick's drug smuggling business. But Ned didn't mention it, except to say that Travis and Mick were in jail now for a long time, which Benny already knew.

'He said he didn't have any vacancies at the moment but he would call me when one came up.'

'That's good. I'll keep my fingers crossed for you.' She hesitated. 'You haven't told me much about what it was like for you in prison. If there's anything you need to tell me, I'm always happy to listen. Often it helps just to talk, to get things out of your mind.'

Benny shook his head. 'Talking about prison will make me feel sad. And

I don't want to be sad, I want to be happy.'

'That's a good philosophy,' Cecilia said, but continued to look at him as if she were waiting for him to say more. What did she want him to say?

'When someone looked like they were going to bash me up, I put on my Clint Eastwood face,' Benny blurted out. 'I pretended I didn't care, because I was stronger than them and could smash them to pieces.'

'Did it work?' Cecilia asked.

Benny nodded. There had been a couple of times it hadn't worked—both times he'd ended up in the prison hospital—but he didn't want to think about those. Or admit it to Cecilia.

'That's brilliant!' she said and gave him another one of those smiles that made his heart flip.

That was only part of the truth. It was the memory of what it felt like to get revenge on Travis after he'd insulted Benny's mother that had really helped him. He would stand tall, put his shoulders back and thrust out his chest, as if putting on an invisible cloak of armour, and look his tormenter in the eye—who would nearly always back down. But he wouldn't tell that to Cecilia—she might think he was bad for beating Travis up in the first place.

'I'm proud of you, Benny.' Cecilia touched his arm lightly then got up from the table, stashing her laptop in her briefcase. 'I've got to go. See you tomorrow.'

Benny watched her leave. His arm tingled where she'd touched it. Later, as he was getting ready for bed, he picked up the photo of his mum where it stood on his bedside table next to her new jewel-encrusted box of ashes. He was sure she didn't feel at home here, but like him, was putting up with it for the time being, until he was allowed to move out.

'I had a good day today, Mum. For the first time ever Lillian mashed the potatoes and they didn't have any lumps in them. And I might have a job. And,' he gave a significant pause, 'I have a new girlfriend. Cecilia. She looks a bit like you, Mum. And she's smart and kind like you. I guess she's not really my girlfriend because I haven't asked her yet, but I know she likes me. She says I'm brilliant and she's very proud of me.'

He kissed the photo. 'Night, Mum.' He placed it gently back on his bedside table. He cleaned his teeth, put on his pyjamas and as he snuggled under his bedclothes, he let his mind drift back to Olivia. He'd often dreamed about her in jail, even though he had come to accept there was no chance of them being together.

After everything he'd done for her, she hadn't appreciated him. Why was she so upset that he killed Lucas when Lucas treated her so badly, and she was leaving the country to get away from him? And to top everything, she'd accused Benny of stalking her. That had hurt the most, along with calling him a pervert. Thankfully the police had dropped the stalking charges due to lack of evidence.

Anyway, Olivia was in the past; he had Cecilia now. Did she already have a boyfriend? Or a husband? Maybe if he crossed his fingers and wished really hard, it would turn out that she didn't. Tomorrow, he'd take the bus to the shops and buy her a bunch of flowers. He felt better than he had for a long time. Things were looking up.

THE END.

Get your e-book of four short crime stories
On The Edge by joining Storey-Lines.

Go to https://storey-lines.com/
for your free copy.

REVIEW

I would really appreciate it if you could take a few minutes to put an honest review of Obsession – A Crime Of The Heart on the site you bought it from. Reviews help other readers to decide whether they will enjoy the book, as well as helping it to gain more visibility and consequently, more sales.

ACKNOWLEDGMENTS

As usual, I have a number of people in my support crew to thank—my partner Aaron, for his love and help with all things formatting and technical, as well as brainstorming plot points, and my family for their moral support, in particular my daughter Emma Hoiberg, for her advice on legal matters in the book.

Many thanks also to my writing buddies without whom I would be lost—my longstanding critique partner Pam Mariko for her constant and invaluable feedback, and Leeza Baric, for reading the manuscript and her insightful comments.

Special thanks to my proofreader Richard Butler, for an excellent job, as usual.

OTHER BOOKS BY ROBIN STOREY

For other books in the Noir Nights series and Robin's stand-alone novels, please visit Storey-Lines http://storey-lines.com or find Robin Storey on Amazon or IngramSpark.

E-books are available at all major e-book retailers.

ABOUT THE AUTHOR

Robin Storey is an indie author who lives on the picturesque Sunshine Coast in Queensland, Australia. She's a former freelance writer who is hooked on writing novels – it's the most challenging, but also the most satisfying thing she's done.

Robin is a certified book nerd and recharges her creative batteries by getting out into nature – hiking and chilling out at the beach.

As far as social media is concerned, Robin mainly hangs out on Facebook, so come on over and like her page.
https://www.facebook.com/RobinStoreywriter

www.ingramcontent.com/pod-product-compliance
Lightning Source LLC
Chambersburg PA
CBHW030436120726
47903CB00003B/989